He Knows

She stopped at a red light and looked over at him, unable to stand the suspense any longer. "What brings you to Chicago?"

Dario turned his head so that their eyes met. There was no mistaking the cold anger in their depths. "Now is neither the time nor the place to discuss it."

Not another word passed between them until they arrived at the hotel. His eyes narrowed on her. "It would appear that we have a lot to talk about, wouldn't it, Jenna?"

"Yes," she sighed resignedly. "I suppose it would."

BRITTANY YOUNG

lives and writes in Racine, Wisconsin. She has traveled to most of the countries which serve as the settings for her romances and finds the research into the language, customs, history, and literature of these countries among the most demanding and rewarding aspects of her writing.

Dear Reader:

I'd like to take this opportunity to thank you for all your support and encouragement of Silhouette Romances.

Many of you write in regularly, telling us what you like best about Silhouette, which authors are your favorites. This is a tremendous help to us as we strive to publish the best contemporary romances possible.

All the romances from Silhouette Books are for you, so enjoy this book and the many stories to come.

Karen Solem
Editor-in-Chief
Silhouette Books

BRITTANY YOUNG
An
Honorable Man

Silhouette Romance

Published by Silhouette Books New York

America's Publisher of Contemporary Romance

Silhouette Books by Brittany Young

Arranged Marriage (ROM #165)
A Separate Happiness (ROM #297)
No Special Consideration (ROM #308)
The Karas Cup (ROM #336)
An Honorable Man (ROM #357)

SILHOUETTE BOOKS
300 E. 42nd St., New York, N.Y. 10017

Copyright © 1985 by Brittany Young
Cover artwork copyright © 1985 by Larry Roibal

Distributed by Pocket Books

ISBN: 0-373-08357-2

First Silhouette Books printing April, 1985

10 9 8 7 6 5 4 3 2 1

Map by Ray Lundgren

An
Honorable Man

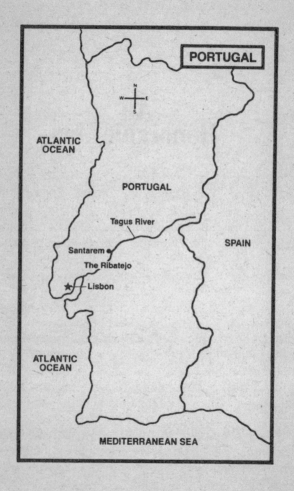

Chapter One

Jenna Hart penciled in the finishing touches on the dress design, then stood back from her drawing board to study the end result with critical hazel eyes. Her blond head tilted this way and that. A dissatisfied frown creased her forehead. "I don't like it."

A young woman walked into the office at that moment, glasses on top of her head, a pencil clamped between her teeth and bolts of colorful cloth spilling over her arms to her knees. "What?" she grunted as she heaved them onto a white couch.

"I said I don't like it. Something's wrong and I can't quite put my finger on it. Come see what you think, Christy."

Christy moved next to her partner in Hart-Windom Fashions, lowered her glasses onto her nose and folded her arms across her somewhat flat chest. "You're right."

"Right?"

She nodded. "Something's wrong."

"Wrong." Jenna sighed. "I was hoping you'd tell me it's perfect and that I was just too punchy to realize it." She studied the board again. "It's something subtle. The basic design is sound."

"The last design of the season is always the hardest, isn't it?" Christy walked over to the coffee pot. "Want a cup?"

"I've already had half the pot. I suppose one more cup won't matter." She walked over to the couch and fingered a bolt of cool, smooth turquoise chintz. "Oh, Christy, this is perfect for the full-skirted suit."

"Ken picked it out."

Ken Hyatt ran the business end of Hart-Windom, allowing Jenna and Christy the freedom to be creative. Jenna designed. Christy sewed.

"The man has taste," Jenna conceded.

Christy glanced at her friend out of the corner of her eye. "So why don't you give him a break and marry him? You're twenty-four years old. Ever since your sister and her husband died six months ago you've completely curtailed your social life to raise their baby. It's not right."

A soft smile curved Jenna's mouth as she thought of ten-month-old Jamie. She wouldn't trade him for the most exciting social life in the world. "You might recall that the year before I got Jamie I had a grand total of three dates."

"What about Ken?"

Jenna took the mug of coffee Christy held out and took a cautious sip of the hot brew. "What about him?"

"If you were to marry, you would give your little nephew a father."

"I would also give myself a husband. And more

particularly, a husband I'm not in love with. Besides, I don't want to get married. Jamie and I are doing fine on our own."

Christy started to press, but Jenna lifted her hand. "Christy, I love you dearly, but you're starting to sound like a broken record. If you're so anxious to see the man married off, marry him yourself."

Christy looked thoughtfully at the mug she cradled in her two hands. "I would, if he'd ask me," she said quietly.

Jenna's hazel eyes widened in dismay. This was the first time she'd had even a hint of Christy's feelings about Ken Hyatt. She put her mug on the white desk and touched her friend's arm in an affectionate gesture of apology. "I didn't know. How long?"

Christy shrugged her shoulders. "Since the day he walked into the office, I suppose."

"And you've kept your feelings to yourself all this time? Why don't you tell the man? He can hardly do anything about them if he doesn't know! You always seem to go out of your way to argue with him."

"Arguing is as good a defense as any. I can't bear the thought of being pitied."

Jenna blinked. "Pitied? What are you talking about?"

"Ken. He treats me like a child most of the time. I can just see him, if he were to find out how I feel about him, smiling benignly and patting me on the head like one of his pets. Poor, poor Christy. She's once again managed to fall in love with a man who's in love with another woman."

"Well that's ridiculous. First of all, the man is only two years older than we are. And he isn't in love with me. He's infatuated. There's an enormous difference between the two, Christy, and you know it. If you were to make even the slightest move in his direction, he wouldn't see me for dust, and you know it as well as I do.''

Christy couldn't help the small smile that curved her mouth. ''I must admit, it's happened before. What was the name of that football player we knew when we were in high school . . . ?''

''Greg Anderson.''

''That's right. It took you a long time to forgive me for stealing him from you.''

''Are you sure I have?''

Christy looked at her sideways. ''Come to think of it, you did remember his name rather quickly.''

''That's right.'' Then suddenly Jenna smiled. ''You're such a goose sometimes, Christy.''

The company secretary opened the door and peered around the corner. ''Am I interrupting anything?''

''No, Sue. What is it?''

''You just got a cable from Portugal.''

Jenna suddenly paled. ''Portugal?''

''Yes. From a man named Dario Montoya. He wants you to pick him up at O'Hare Airport, the private plane terminal, at eight P.M. sharp. That doesn't give you much time.'' The secretary glanced at her watch. ''It's already seven fifteen. If you leave right now you might just make it.''

Jenna's slender frame leaned heavily against the desk as the door closed behind her secretary. Christy pushed her glasses back on top of her head and frowned at her friend. ''Who on earth is Dario Montoya? And isn't that little Jamie's last name?''

''Yes, it's Jamie's last name, and Dario is his uncle.''

"Well, what do you suppose he's coming to Chicago for?"

"I don't know, but I hope to heaven it isn't to see Jamie."

Christy was confused. "I don't understand."

Jenna agitatedly tapped her balled fist on the desk. "Because I didn't tell the Montoya family Jamie even existed."

Christy's mouth dropped open. "Why on earth not? This Dario person has a right to know his dead brother left behind a child. Not to tell him, or the rest of the family, is cruel. That's not like you, Jenna. Not at all!"

Jenna paced, her hands deep in the pockets of her gathered grape cotton skirt. "Believe me, Christy, I've had nightmares about that. But my sister asked *me* to raise Jamie. I have nothing in writing. Just a deathbed plea. I gave her my word. I knew if I told the Montoya family about him they'd take him away from me."

"You could have fought them in court."

Jenna pushed her hair away from her face. "Not a chance. I mean, our company is doing well. You and I are more than comfortable. But the Montoyas have millions, and believe me when I say that they would have spent every last penny of it to get Jamie."

"You sound as though you know them personally."

"Not them." Her voice softened. "Only Dario. He's the oldest son and head of the family." Her eyes met Christy's. "He can be ruthless when it suits him."

"Sounds fascinating to me."

A corner of Jenna's mouth lifted reluctantly. "He can be that, too."

There was something about Jenna when she spoke of

this man that captured Christy's attention. "Exactly how well do you know him?"

"Well enough to think I'd fallen in love with him three years ago when he was in town visiting his brother."

Christy looked offended. "We've been friends since kindergarten and you never once mentioned him to me."

"I never mentioned Dario to anyone. It was strictly a case of unrequited love. And very personal," she added.

Christy studied her friend closely. "Is that the *real* reason you never told him about Jamie?"

"You mean to get back at him?"

Christy nodded.

"No," Jenna told her with quiet sincerity. "My reasons were just as I told you. I must admit, I was heartbroken at the time. He's really a very special man. But how can you hold against a man the fact that he can't return your affection? It was hardly Dario's fault."

"It sounds like you're not over him yet."

"Does any woman ever get over the first man she falls in love with?" Jenna asked.

Christy smiled reminiscently. "No, I guess not, come to think of it." She glanced at her watch. "Listen, girl, if you're going to meet his plane you'd better get moving."

Jenna picked her purse up from the desk and fit it under her arm. "You're right. It could be that he doesn't know anything about Jamie, and if that's the case," she crossed her fingers for luck, "I don't want him showing up at my apartment, do I?"

She headed for the door, but turned back. "Listen, Christy. Do me a favor and call Mrs. Braun, will you? She expected to stay with Jamie late tonight, but tell her I might be later than I anticipated."

"Don't worry. I'll take care of it."

But Jenna was already on her way to the underground parking garage. She tossed her purse onto the passenger seat of her forest green Jaguar sedan and climbed behind the wheel. The hand holding the keys was poised over the ignition. But suddenly she clenched her jaw and closed her eyes. "Please," she whispered, "don't let him have come here to take Jamie from me."

The trip took half an hour. She parked in front of the airport terminal and put her flashers on, then walked quickly inside and down a long, busy corridor. She hadn't the faintest idea at which gate he would be arriving, but before she had a chance to ask, she saw him.

Jenna stopped walking. He looked much the same as he had the last time they'd met. His hair was short and black and combed neatly away from his handsomely carved face. His skin was permanently bronzed from a lifetime spent on his ranch in Portugal.

Dario was a tall man with a muscular build that even the dark suit he had on couldn't disguise. He carried his leather travel bag hooked on a finger over his shoulder. She was vaguely aware of women turning to stare as he passed. She ran the tip of her tongue over dry lips. The knot in her stomach grew larger as his strides brought him to her.

There was no smile as he looked down at her. His tawny eyes were cool and her heart sank. "Hello, Dario."

Those eyes took their time as they looked her over very thoroughly. "I wasn't sure you would be here."

Jenna refused to lower her gaze. "I almost wasn't. Your cable didn't arrive until about an hour ago."

"Where are you parked?" he asked, obviously in no mood for small talk.

"In front." They headed toward the exit. Dario opened

the rear door of the Jaguar and tossed his travel bag onto the backseat while Jenna climbed behind the wheel.

She drummed her fingers nervously on the steering wheel while he got settled, then put the car into gear and pulled onto the road. She skillfully maneuvered their way through the heavy evening traffic, intensely aware of the man seated next to her. There was an uncomfortable silence. But then Jenna broke it. "What hotel are you staying at?"

"I have a suite at the Palmer House."

She stopped at a red light and looked over at him, unable to stand the suspense any longer. "What brings you to Chicago?"

Dario turned his head so that their eyes met head on. There was no mistaking the cold anger in their depths. "Now is neither the time nor the place to discuss it."

Jenna swallowed hard. He *knew!* But how? The light changed and she put the car into motion. Not another word passed between them until they arrived at the hotel.

Dario took the keys out of the ignition before she could and handed them to the doorman who approached the car. Then he looked back at Jenna. "You can wait in my suite while I shower and change. We'll have dinner in the hotel and talk." His eyes narrowed on her. "And it would appear that we have a lot to talk about, wouldn't it, Jenna?"

"Yes," she sighed resignedly. "I suppose it would."

She followed him into the hotel and waited with a sort of doomed patience while he checked in. That done, he carelessly put his hand against the small of her back to guide her through the elegant lobby to the elevator. They rode up in silence, with Jenna taking surreptitious glances at Dario from the corner of her eye in an attempt to gauge the extent of his anger. It was for nothing, though. He was as unfathomable as she remembered.

Once in the suite, he flipped on the lights and walked straight through. "Make yourself at home. I won't be long," he informed her before closing the bedroom door behind him.

Jenna wandered aimlessly to the large windows and stared out on the twinkling lights of Chicago. At the moment she had a weight like a brick on her chest. Breathing was difficult. She couldn't remember ever dreading a dinner the way she was dreading this one. But of one thing she was certain. He wasn't going to get Jamie without a fight. She straightened her shoulders and defiantly lifted her chin.

That was how Dario found her when he finally emerged from the bedroom, showered and changed. He opened the door for her. "Shall we?"

She swept past him into the hall. The man's enigmatic eyes softened on her for just a moment as he closed the door. He could well imagine what was going on in her mind. But he had no intention of making it any easier on her.

Within minutes they were seated at a secluded table where they could talk without being observed. Dario ordered dinner and wine for both of them. Ordinarily Jenna would have protested, but this time she held her tongue. She had more important things to worry about than what she was having for dinner.

Still they sat in silence. The waiter brought their wine, poured it and left. Then Dario looked at her—really looked at her—for the first time since they'd gotten out of the car. The muscles in her stomach tightened in readiness for the blow.

"You have changed since the last time we met," he surprised her by saying.

She breathed in relief at the reprieve. "I'm older."

His eyes rested thoughtfully on her lovely face. "No. It's more than that." He leaned back in his chair. "I understand your business has become quite successful."

This was a topic she could really sink her teeth into, and she relaxed a little. "Yes, it has. Christy and I have both worked hard to make it that way."

"Christy? She is the Windom in Hart-Windom?"

"Yes, that's right. I'm sorry. I forgot that you two didn't meet the last time you were in Chicago." She relaxed a little more. Maybe he didn't know after all.

"And there is a man involved, I believe?"

She nodded her blonde head. "Ken Hyatt. He manages the company for us."

"Your picture has shown up in several magazines along with articles about your rather surprising success. I've followed your career with interest."

"Ken tries to keep our name in the press. It's good for business."

Dario grew thoughtful as his tawny eyes rested on this woman he had fallen in love with so fast and so hard all those years ago. If it was physically possible to hunger for the sight of someone, that was how he felt about Jenna Hart. "I have thought of you often over the years," he finally told her.

Jenna returned the look, wondering what was going on behind those enigmatic eyes of his. "I've thought of you as well, especially when Carlos and Caroline died." A little of the hurt she'd felt at the time crept into her voice. "You never even called me. Attorneys handled everything."

"That was because of me, Jenna, not you."

A small frown creased her brow. "I don't understand. We parted friends, you and I, no matter what went on between you and Carlos. At least I thought we had."

"We were friends."

"Then why didn't you at least call when they died? I lost a sister. You lost a brother. We could have helped each other."

"I couldn't call you. I couldn't see you. And at the moment I haven't the emotional energy to explain." His eyes examined each and every feature of Jenna's face. He had a way of making a woman feel as though she were the only person in the room, even if there were a hundred others in it. She remembered that quality from their time together before his brother had married her sister. She had always felt special when she was with Dario.

Dario's gaze grew more intense until finally Jenna had to lower her eyes, afraid he would read the guilt she carried in her heart over the secret she had kept from him all these months.

But Dario would have none of that. He leaned forward and took her chin between his thumb and forefinger, forcing her to look at him. Even before he spoke, Jenna knew what he was going to say. "You should have told me that my brother had fathered a child before he died."

Jenna took a deep breath. "How did you find out?"

"A copy of the birth certificate was among Carlos' things." His tawny eyes grew dark. "I had a right to know."

Jenna closed her eyes for a long moment, then slowly opened them, forcing herself to look at him. "Yes," she agreed quietly. "You did."

"And yet you lied."

She started to protest, but he cut her off.

"You did. Every day that passed without your telling me about Jamie, you lied." His voice was calm, but the truth of his words sliced through her.

Jenna's throat closed so tightly it made swallowing difficult. "You're right." Her voice wasn't much more than a whisper, but she didn't drop her eyes.

He let go of her chin and leaned back in his chair, eyes still narrowed on her. "Why?"

Jenna sat quietly for several moments. "I didn't want you to take Jamie away from me."

"I am the boy's uncle."

She looked up sharply. "An uncle with whom his father had refused to speak for over three years."

Dario studied the rich red liquid in the long-stemmed glass. "It is true there was a rift between Carlos and myself which was never healed." He picked up the glass and swirled the wine before taking a drink. "To my everlasting regret."

Jenna leaned back in her chair also, though she knew the battle was far from over. "Why were you so against your brother marrying Caroline?"

"I had my reasons."

"Caroline always thought it was because we didn't have money, or even family, for that matter, except for each other."

He smiled but there was no amusement in it. "Caroline was wrong."

"I know that. I told her so."

He sipped his wine and eyed her over the rim. "And how did you get so smart?"

Jenna lifted her shoulders in a delicate shrug. "I guess I

felt I knew you better than she did. You didn't strike me as a man who would like or dislike a person based on a bank balance.''

He said nothing.

Jenna leaned forward. "Dario, why were you against the marriage?''

His eyes rested on her softly parted mouth. "It makes no difference anymore, Jenna. They're dead.''

"But I'm not, and it's important to me.''

He leaned forward also and toyed thoughtfully with his wine glass for a moment until he came to a decision. "Carlos was already betrothed to a Portuguese woman when he met your sister. I know that in the United States a broken engagement is a common thing. But not in Portugal. A promise of marriage is tantamount to the actual marriage. His fiancee's name was Elisa, and she was pregnant with his child when he married your sister.''

Her expressive eyes filled with sympathy. "Oh, no. I didn't know any of this. And I'm sure Caroline didn't either. She would never have married Carlos under those circumstances.''

"From what I knew of your sister, I'd guess you are right. I liked her, and it was easy for me to see why Carlos loved her so.''

Jenna studied him thoughtfully. "When you came here before the marriage, it was to try to get him to go home to Elisa, wasn't it?''

"That's right.'' And that's when I met you, he finished silently.

"What did Elisa finally end up doing?''

Again that muscle in his jaw worked. "She married me.''

Jenna was sure she hadn't heard right. "What?"

He lifted a dark brow at her. "Which word didn't you hear?"

She ignored his sarcasm. "But why?"

"It was the only honorable solution."

Jenna was appalled. It didn't occur to her to wonder about the violence of her reaction. "Honorable solution? It's barbaric! I'm sorry that your brother fell out of love with her, and I'm sorry for the unwitting part my sister played, but for you to take your brother's place . . ." She shook her blond head. "That's unbelievable."

"And what would you have had her do?" he asked coolly.

"Women have been known to raise children alone. You're looking at one."

"Jamie is not your illegitimate child. There is no tolerance of illegitimacy in Portugal. Perhaps in years to come, but not now. Besides, Elisa was never as strong as you apparently are."

"Was?" His use of the past tense caught her ear.

"She was thrown from a horse eight weeks ago and killed."

"Oh God," she whispered. Without thinking, only wanting to ease the pain she saw suddenly etched on his face, Jenna reached across the table and covered his hand comfortingly with her own. "I'm so sorry."

Dario stared at her hand, then slowly turned his palm up and twined his fingers through hers, drawing comfort from her.

"What about the child?" she finally asked.

"Elisa miscarried shortly after the wedding."

He disengaged his hand from hers and sat back in his chair. "I didn't come here to talk to you about this. I came here to discuss Jamie.'' He frowned. ''I should tell you that when I first found out about Jamie, I was angry. Angry and hurt. But I've had time to think about your actions now and I understand why you did what you did. If the situation were reversed, I probably would have done the same thing.''

Relief washed over her, but it was short-lived. ''Thank you.''

''But I am still going to take Jamie back to Portugal with me.''

She looked up at him sharply. ''No!''

''Yes. He has a great-grandmother there who already loves him, sight unseen. And he has his future.''

''What future?''

''Upon the death of his father, Jamie inherited a good portion of the family ranch and business. You would deny him this?''

''Well, no, of course not . . .''

''But that is exactly what you are doing. He should be raised as a Montoya. He *is* a Montoya. He should grow up on the ranch he will one day own and learn to love it.''

''But at what cost?'' Her distress on the child's behalf was clear in every syllable.

Dario caught her hand again and held it firmly in his. ''He will be as my own son, Jenna. He will be loved and nurtured.''

''But he thinks of me as his mother now. And so soon after losing his own, to be taken away from me too . . .'' Her voice was full of dismay. ''He needs to be secure right now. He needs me.''

Dario leaned back in his chair, his eyes on her. ''I agree.'' He paused. ''I have a proposition for you.''

''Proposition?'' she asked curiously.

"Come to Portugal. Live in my home with the child. Raise him as you are doing now."

Jenna blinked. "In Portugal? I don't think you fully understand the situation, Dario," she explained. "I have a business here. A good one. I can't just stop in the middle of everything and move to Portugal. People are depending on me."

"Why not? You have a partner and an associate who manages things for both of you."

"True," she admitted. "I only design the clothes."

He shrugged his broad shoulders. "Is there some reason why that can't be done in a place other than Chicago?"

She was caught off-guard. "Well, there would be the problem of transporting my designs from Portugal to here. And we put on two fashion shows a year. I'd have to be here for those."

He inclined his dark head. "You can use my jet to transport your creations, and yourself, whenever the need arises."

Jenna was skeptical of all this good will. "Why are you being so generous?"

"That's simple enough. I want what is best for Jamie. He needs you. But," he leaned forward to drive home his point all the more clearly, "if I have to take him without you, I will. With regret—but I will."

They stopped talking while dinner was served. When the waiter had gone, Jenna looked across the table. "How long have I got to think it over?"

"Until the day after tomorrow. Jamie and I are leaving then."

"The day after tomorrow!" Her objection was so loud that the other diners turned in their seats to stare. "I can't possibly be ready by then!" she said, more quietly this time. "There are things to take care of—my apartment to sublet, a design to finish, packing—I could go on and on."

"You could come at a later time, when your affairs are settled."

"I don't think so."

"So your decision is no."

"No!" This time she caught herself. "I mean," she said more calmly, "No, my decision isn't no. It's . . ." She pushed her hair away from her face. "Oh, I don't know what it is. What's the hurry? Why can't you give me a little more time?"

"Jamie's great-grandmother is an old woman. She hasn't been well for a very long time. Carlos' death was hard on her. I would like her to have the pleasure of knowing his son—her great-grandson—before she dies. And," he added, "her birthday is the day after tomorrow. This is the nicest gift anyone could give her."

She shook her head. "I'm having trouble taking all of this in," she said quietly.

Dario inclined his head toward her plate. "Eat. We'll talk more later."

She picked at her food, not really seeing it. Her mind was in turmoil. To leave the United States, just like that! Could she do it? And if he was taking Jamie the day after tomorrow, that would be a critical time for the baby. She couldn't let him go off with a man he'd never even seen before, uncle or not. He'd be frightened. If she were going, it was important that she go when Jamie did—when he needed her most.

She was completely unaware of Dario's eyes watching the emotions chasing across her expressive face. When the waiter arrived and asked if she were finished, she gave him a little smile and pushed the untouched plate toward him.

"No," Dario said. "She hasn't finished yet."

Jenna frowned at him. "Yes, she has."

Dario gave the waiter a look and the man left. Jenna lifted a shapely brow. "I should perhaps explain to you that I don't take well to people telling me what to do, and with you, I reached my limit quite a while ago."

"Then why are you still sitting here?"

"Because I don't appear to have much of a choice, do I?" She drummed her fingers on the table. "Would you consider sharing custody?"

"You mean having the child spend six months with me and six months with you?"

She nodded, but her straight nose wrinkled. "I'm reaching," she admitted. "That wouldn't work. He needs *one* home."

"At least we are agreed on that."

"As I said," Jenna sighed, "you leave me no choice."

He inclined his dark head. "Another thing on which we are agreed."

Jenna felt tears welling in her eyes, but quickly blinked them away. It was horrible to feel so helpless. "What time will you be picking us up?"

His heart caught at the tremor in her voice. He reached across the table and captured her hand in his, forcing her to look into his eyes. "Portugal isn't the end of the world, you know. It's a beautiful place. I think, if you give yourself a chance, you'll come to love it as I do, and as Jamie will. Or it may turn out that once you've met the rest of the family, you'll feel secure enough about the child's future with us to leave him in our hands."

Dario Montoya was a man who inspired trust and

confidence. Some of his assurance flowed from him to her. "Anything is possible, I suppose," she conceded.

A corner of his carved mouth lifted as he gazed at her. "That's what makes life interesting. Now eat some of your dinner."

She surprised herself by doing as he asked and actually managed to enjoy a few bites. After dabbing her mouth delicately with her napkin, she put it on the table next to her plate, but her eyes were on the man across from her. "You look tired," she remarked, surprised to find that she actually cared.

"I *am* tired, Jenna."

The way he said her name with the merest hint of an accent delighted her ear. She moved her chair back. "Well, I'll let you get some sleep, then. If we're leaving the day after tomorrow, I have a thousand things to do."

He put some money on the table without waiting for the check and rose. "Very well. And to answer your earlier question, we'll be leaving around eleven o'clock."

Together they walked from the restaurant to the lobby. Dario placed his hand casually at the small of her back. Men had done that before when she walked with them and she had thought nothing of it, but with Dario it was different. She was *aware* of his touch.

"There's something else I need to ask you," he told her while they waited for the doorman to get her car. "Did you find among Caroline's things her certificate of marriage to my brother?"

Jenna thought for a moment. "As a matter of fact, I didn't. Why?"

"I was just curious." He paused thoughtfully. "Were you a witness to their marriage?"

"I'm afraid not. They simply took off one weekend,

came back a few days later and announced that they were married. I don't even know where they went.''

The doorman returned with her car and Jenna turned to Dario and extended her hand. He held it in both of his. She looked up at him with a smile, but as their eyes met, her smile faded. She remembered their parting three years ago. She remembered the grief which had filled her when she'd watched him drive away for the last time. The pain she had felt showed in her lovely face, and the man saw it.

''Goodnight, Jenna,'' he said softly.

Dario watched until the tail lights of her car disappeared around a corner, then he took a deep breath and looked up at the starless sky. ''Ah, Jenna,'' he breathed.

Chapter Two

Jenna raced home, nudging the posted speeds occasionally, but more often passing them entirely. There was so much to do and so little time in which to do it.

She pulled to a screeching halt in front of her comfortable apartment building, then stood in the lobby impatiently poking the elevator button again and again, as though that would make it come faster. It was already past midnight.

She found Mrs. Braun sitting on the couch watching television and doing needlepoint. "How is Jamie?" she asked, tossing her purse and keys on the hall table.

The babysitter put the needlepoint into a cloth bag next to the couch. "Sleeping like a dream. I just checked on him a few minutes ago."

"That's good. Thank you." She dropped onto the couch next to her. "Listen, Mrs. Braun, I know you've had a long day, but I'm going to ask you to do another favor for me. It's a big one."

The woman patted her hand affectionately. "Anything, dear. You know that."

"I do know that, and I appreciate it, believe me," she said gratefully. "What I need now is for you to pack all of Jamie's clothes and whatever toys you can fit into the suitcases you'll find in the hall closet."

The middle-aged woman's eyes widened in distress. "Why? What's going on? Is everything all right?"

"Oh, yes! I didn't mean to frighten you. It's just that everything is happening so quickly I haven't the time for subtlety. I probably never mentioned this to you, but Jamie has an uncle living in Portugal."

"But I thought you were his only relative!" she said in surprise.

Jenna smiled, but there was little amusement in it. "Yes, well, I never told you otherwise. At any rate, this uncle arrived in Chicago tonight. We just finished dinner. It would appear that Jamie and I are returning with him to Portugal the day after tomorrow."

"To live?" Mrs. Braun asked in disbelief.

"For the time being. We'll have to see how it goes and whether I think this uncle's ranch is a good place to raise a child."

Mrs. Braun shook her head. "I can't believe you're doing this."

"I'm as amazed as you are," Jenna sympathized. "When I awoke this morning I never dreamed any of this was going to happen. But my hands are tied. If I balk on this Dario could take Jamie away from me altogether. At least this way I get to be with him. And considering what I did, Dario is being generous. I honestly believe he has Jamie's best interests at heart.''

Mrs. Braun rubbed her forehead in bewilderment. "I'm having trouble taking all this in."

"I know," Jenna agreed. Mrs. Braun couldn't have taken better care of Jamie or loved him more, if he were her own grandson. "I'm sorry to have to throw this at you so suddenly, but if you could pack his things, it would be an enormous help. I still have to drive back to the office to clear up my unfinished work, not to mention telling Christy about our new long-distance arrangement."

"Oh, my," Mrs. Braun clicked her tongue. "I don't expect Miss Windom will be pleased."

"I don't expect Miss Windom has much of a choice. And frankly neither do I."

Mrs. Braun took a deep breath and patted Jenna's knee as she rose from the couch. "Well, you take care of your business, and I'll take care of Jamie's packing. Don't you worry about a thing. And if you want me to spend the night, that's no problem either."

Jenna hugged her. She genuinely liked Mrs. Braun. "I knew I could count on you. Thank you. I haven't any idea how long I'll be." She was rushed, but even that couldn't break a habit she had developed over the past six months. Quietly, she tiptoed into Jamie's room and looked down at the sweetly sleeping child. His short, dark curls were shadows against his white pillow. With a gentle hand she smoothed the hair away from his soft cheek and kissed it, then laid her cheek against his for just a moment, the tiniest smile curving her mouth as she inhaled the delicious scent of a clean baby.

She pulled the blanket up a little and watched as he

moved. But he didn't wake. "I love you," she whispered before she tiptoed out and shut the door behind her. Then more quickly she strode to her purse and keys. "Oh, Mrs. Braun—one other thing. Would you please call Christy and ask her to meet me at the office? And tell her it's urgent."

The woman nodded, and Jenna was on her way.

She arrived at the office in record time. It was an eerie hour to be alone in the tall building. So deserted. Every creak was distorted and magnified by the surrounding silence. But she had things to do and couldn't let that worry her.

The first thing she did was find a rubber band in her desk and use it to hold her hair away from her face in a heavy ponytail. Then she waded through the mail and answered what needed to be answered and referred to Ken and Christy what needed to be referred.

"Jenna! Where are you?" It was Christy's voice.

"In my office."

She walked in and flopped tiredly in a chair across the desk from her partner. "What on earth is going on? I got this mysterious call from your babysitter telling me to meet you here. And may I further say that I was sound asleep."

Jenna leaned back in her chair and rubbed her eyes. "I'm really sorry, Christy, but this couldn't wait until tomorrow."

"Does it have something to do with that Dario Montoya person you met tonight at the airport."

"Everything, I'm afraid."

Christy lifted an inquiring brow.

"He wants Jamie to live in Portugal."

"Without you?"

Jenna paused as she looked at her friend, wondering what kind of reaction her next words would generate. "With me."

Christy's eyes widened, and then she shook her head. "But that's impossible. I hope you told him that it's simply impossible. You have a business here. We've really gotten it off the ground in the last two years. We're getting a reputation—a good one. We can't afford to upset the chemistry we have going for us with our customers right now." She was still shaking her head. "I'm afraid it's out of the question."

Jenna felt like a heel, dumping this on her partner so suddenly. "I've thought it over, Christy. I know it's not as satisfactory as my working here, but I can design clothes in Portugal, and he's agreed to let me use his jet whenever it's necessary to fly my designs to you, and to bring me to Chicago whenever you need me. That should help a lot. What do you think?"

Christy just sat there trying to take it all in. "Jenna, this is crazy. You come into the office every day as it is, and look how busy you are. The shows take months to plan, not days. You do a lot more around here than design the clothes."

"I understand that, but we're all going to have to adjust. And if we need to hire extra help, then that's what we'll have to do. It's very important that I stay with Jamie. He needs me . . . and to be honest, I need him."

Christy knew how Jenna felt about Jamie. To give him up would be like giving up her own son. How could she fight something like that? Christy studied her friend's lovely face. "You've already made up your mind, haven't you?"

"I have. But it's important to me that I have your okay."

Christy raked her fingers through her hair. "Look," she finally told her, "I'm not wild about the idea. The way we're set up now has worked perfectly, and as the saying goes, if it ain't broke, don't fix it. But I know you can't lose Jamie. If you have to work in Portugal to keep him, then so be it. The *two* of us are Hart-Windom Fashions. Without either one of us, the business will go under."

"Agreed."

Christy raised her hands. "Then that's it. We'll hire someone to handle any correspondence which doesn't need an answer directly from you and to make the fashion show arrangements, and we'll hope for the best." She watched her friend thoughtfully. "You know, though, Ken isn't going to take this nearly as well as I have."

"Ken isn't my partner. And if he doesn't like it, I'm sorry, but it's really not my problem."

Christy lifted an expressive brow. She wasn't used to hearing Jenna say things like that. "Well, aren't you the tough cookie tonight?"

A wry smile touched Jenna's mouth. "Just a tired cookie. And when I get tired, my tact is the first thing to bite the dust. You should know that better than anyone."

Christy exhaled a long breath. "Do you have much left to do?"

Jenna waved toward her drawing table. "I want to get that design finished."

Christy nodded. "You have to. We need it in two days."

"Believe me, I know."

"Then I'll let you get to it." Christy got to her feet and

walked around the desk to hug her friend. "I'm going to miss you so much."

Jenna hugged her back. "I'll miss you, too."

"Do you want me to stay here with you tonight? Maybe I could help with some things."

"Thanks, but no. I think everything is pretty much under control."

"I could come in tomorrow ... ."

"No, really. It's all right."

"Okay." But still Christy hesitated, loathe to leave. "You call me whenever you can."

"Whenever I can and probably more than I should."

With a final wave over her shoulder, Christy left, and with a tired sigh, Jenna sat in front of her drawing board, pencils in hand and pushed everything else from her mind so she could concentrate on her work. The hours sped along, and by the time she was finished the sun had risen and the city of Chicago was stirring.

But the design was a good one.

Wearily she packed up the materials she needed to take to Portugal and drove back to her apartment just as the Saturday morning traffic was starting. Mrs. Braun met her at the door with a sympathetic smile. "Did you get everything done that you wanted?"

"Not everything. Can you stay for another twenty-four hours? I have a lot of personal things to clear up today, and then I really think I should go back to the office tonight. I wasn't able to get all of my paperwork done."

"Of course I can. Just let me make a quick trip home for a change of clothes." She looked Jenna over. "And I think you should try to take a nap while I'm gone."

"I will. I can hardly keep my eyes open."

Mrs. Braun picked up her purse and headed out the door. "I'll be right back."

After her nap, Jenna quickly showered and changed her clothes and then sat on the couch and made a very organized list of things she had to do. Then she spent the rest of the day doing them. Once again she worked all night at the office, and when dawn arrived on Sunday, she was able to lean back in her chair with a satisfied sigh. Finished.

When Jenna finally got back to her apartment, Mrs. Braun met her at the door. "Well?"

"I'm ready." Jenna collapsed prone onto the couch. "Where's Jamie?"

"He's been up, bathed, breakfasted, dressed and now he's napping."

"Napping." She sighed enviously. "Sounds like heaven to me. I still have to pack."

"No, you don't." She busily collected her sewing and got ready to leave. "I thought that since I was taking care of Jamie's things, I might as well take care of yours as well. Needless to say I only packed your summer clothes."

"Mrs. Braun, I could kiss you," Jenna said in grateful surprise. "You have no idea how I was dreading that."

"Well, then, as a thank you I would appreciate a letter telling me how the two of you are getting on in Portugal."

"I promise."

She opened the door, but looked back at Jenna one more time. "And you get some sleep before that uncle of Jamie's gets here."

"I will."

When the door shut behind her, Jenna closed her eyes, intending to rest for just a moment. But the moment stretched. She slept so deeply that she didn't hear the knock. Nor did she hear Dario open the unlocked door and walk in. He stood quietly looking down at her for a long time, his hard face full of a tenderness which would have amazed Jenna, had she seen it. Reluctantly, he bent to touch her shoulder. "Jenna, it is time to wake."

Still asleep, she frowned and turned onto her side.

At that the man smiled and sat beside her. His hand gently pushed the heavy blond hair off her cheek. She looked a little crumpled, as though she'd been up all night. "Come on," he coaxed. "You can sleep on the jet."

His words began soaking into her consciousness. With a groan, she turned onto her back and slowly opened her heavy-lidded eyes. "Good morning." Her arms stretched high over her head.

"Hello." He continued looking at her. "Are you ready?"

"Is it time? So soon?" She looked at her watch. "I must have fallen asleep." She looked up at him. "Do I have time to shower and change?"

"A few minutes." He took her hands and pulled her into a sitting position.

"Thank you." She yawned again and shook her head apologetically. "I'm sorry, but I had a long night." She got up and walked toward her bedroom. "I'll hurry with my shower." But Jenna stopped in the doorway and turned. *"Our* nephew is asleep in his crib, through that door." She inclined her head toward the baby's room.

The grooves in his cheeks deepened at her emphasis on the word "our." "Thank you."

She returned his smile and closed the door behind her.

She showered quickly, letting cold water bite into her skin, then stepped out and into her short white terrycloth robe. All in all, she was feeling much better about going to Portugal than she had been last night. She still wasn't happy about it, but feeling sorry for herself wasn't going to change anything. There came a time when one simply had to make the best of a bad situation.

"Jenna! Come out here this instant!" a voice demanded from the living room.

She pulled the robe more tightly around her and securely tied the belt. Walking into the living room, she saw an angry Ken Hyatt standing stiffly in the middle of the floor and Dario relaxing on the couch while Jamie climbed all over him.

She smiled at Ken, ready for the worst. "Hi. I take it you've talked to Christy."

"I have." His light blue eyes narrowed on her attire. "For heaven's sake, put some clothes on."

"Oh, Ken, don't be ridiculous. You've seen me in less than this at the beach."

"And him?" He dipped his head toward the other man.

Dario, with a deliberateness that took Jenna's breath away, looked her over, from her long legs to the damp tendrils of hair curling on her forehead. A corner of his handsome mouth lifted. "I have no complaint."

She suddenly felt exposed, and to her chagrin, she felt her cheeks grow pink. But she refused to run and hide like some teenager. "Ken, we're in a bit of a hurry so if there's something you want to say, please get on with it."

He ran his fingers through his sandy hair. "This is crazy. I can't believe you're just up and leaving. I have to hear it from you myself."

Dario set Jamie on the floor and he toddled to Jenna. She picked him up and gently kissed him on the forehead. "Hello, sweetheart." Then she brought her attention back to Ken. "There's no reason to get all upset. Christy and I talked about this last night. There are going to be some obvious problems with the new arrangement, but nothing which we can't work around."

"But you can't run a business from there."

"Ken," she said reasonably, "I don't run the business when I'm *here*. You do."

"And if I need to consult with you on something? Which I need to do nearly every day," he added for good measure.

"Call me." She glanced at Dario, her eyes alight. "You *do* have telephones, don't you?"

"Oh," he dismissed, "that technology has been available in Portugal for months now."

Jamie struggled in her arms and she put him on the floor. He toddled back to his uncle. A bond was already growing between them, and if she'd had any doubts about what she was doing, the look on Dario's face when he laughingly lifted Jamie high over his head put an end to them.

She looked back at Ken. "I think that takes care of things. I'll still be producing my designs. The only difference is that I won't be coming to the office."

He was really deeply offended. "That's all you have to say about it?"

"That's all there is." He looked so downcast that she put her hand on his arm and gave it an affectionate squeeze. "Ken, it'll work out, believe me. I'll be back before you know it to help with the winter show."

He relented. "I'm sorry, Jenna. It's just that I'm going to miss you."

"I'll miss you, too. You're a good friend." She walked him to the door. "You know," she said confidentially, "Christy's going to need your support more than ever now. She depends on you. She always has." And it was true. There were times during the intense pressure of the fashion shows when she was sure that if it hadn't been for Ken's intense hovering, Christy would have fallen apart. And the beauty of it was that Ken was one of those men who needed to be needed. This was a match made by the gods.

"Do you really think so?" he asked.

Men could be so obtuse at times, she thought as she kissed his cheek. "I really think so."

His eyes rested resignedly on her face. "Well, I've said what I came to say. I only hope the business doesn't suffer because of this decision."

"It's not going to suffer. You and Christy can handle it."

Ken sighed. His face softened as he reached out a gentle hand and touched her cheek. "I meant what I said before about missing you. And that's personal, not business."

"You're a good friend."

He glanced over her head at the man on the couch and lowered his voice. "I've always wanted to be more than that to you."

"I know."

"No hope?"

She covered his hand warmly with hers. "No. You're my friend, and that's important to me, but that's as far as it goes."

He inclined his head. "All right. I had to ask." He

raised his voice to it's normal level. "You take care of yourself."

"I'll be fine."

After she closed the door, she stood there for a moment, oblivious to her surroundings.

"It's time to leave. You'd better get dressed." Dario's voice cut through the silence.

Jenna jumped and turned. "I forgot you were here."

"I know." He eyed her robe as he bounced a delighted Jamie on his knee.

Jenna tugged it self-consciously into a more secure position and walked quickly to her room.

She came out a few minutes later dressed in a gathered white skirt and a lavender and white striped blouse with banded cuffs. Her golden hair was held away from her face by lavender combs. "I'm ready."

Dario eyed her appreciatively as he handed Jamie to her. "That's almost as nice as the robe. I'll get the luggage."

"It'll take more than one trip." Jenna kept staring at him. She didn't mean to—in fact, most of the time she didn't realize she was doing it—but every once in awhile she'd catch herself and force her eyes away. She liked the way he looked. She liked the way he moved. She even liked the scent of his aftershave.

But what really intrigued Jenna was her reaction to him. Just the fact that she *had* one.

Dario came back for the last of the luggage. Jamie put his dark head on Jenna's shoulder with a sigh and she pressed her lips against his curls. Dario watched them quietly. "Now I see why you two come as a package deal."

She smiled over the baby's head. "Isn't he beautiful?"

"Almost unbelievably." But he was looking at Jenna, not the baby. The dark gaze nonplussed her and she suddenly felt her heart thumping erratically beneath her breast.

"Come." His eyes still on her, Dario held open the apartment door. "Let us go home."

Jenna inconspicuously studied him on the way to the airport. He seemed more rested than he had the other night. More relaxed.

Dario turned his head and their eyes met. A corner of his mouth lifted. "You're taking this upheaval in your life much better than I expected."

"I'm a resilient woman."

"So it would appear. That's a nice quality."

"Thank you."

He turned his attention back to the road, but she kept her eyes on him. He noticed. "Are you trying to figure out if I have any nice qualities?" he asked dryly.

A dimple lightly creased her left cheek. "I already know you have some. I'm just wondering what the rest of them are."

His eyes met hers again. "Not only resilient, but charming."

"I have my moments."

"And what if there are no others?"

"No other nice qualities? Then I'll be greatly disappointed."

"Oh, we can't have that."

"I like your attitude."

At that, the man laughed. "Oh, Jenna," he finally said, "I had forgotten how you used to make me laugh."

She didn't respond, but continued studying the fascinating man who had so unexpectedly reappeared in her life—and wondered what the future held.

"What are you thinking?" he asked, glancing at her as he maneuvered the car through traffic.

She hesitated. "I was more or less wondering what role you're destined to play in my life."

"A prominent one," he answered.

"You're very confident."

"That's right."

And she liked his confidence. There wasn't anything more boring to her than a wishy-washy person, male or female.

Jamie began jabbering baby talk in the back seat and Jenna turned her attention to him, but her thoughts were still on the man next to her.

"Has it been difficult for you, being a single mother?" he asked.

Jenna turned back in her seat. "A little. My work is very demanding of my time. I think Jamie gets short-changed on occasion, particularly when we're getting ready for a fashion show. But I was very lucky to find Mrs. Braun. She's become his own personal grandmother."

"What about later in your life, when you have children of your own. Will you still work?"

She delicately lifted her shoulders. "I don't know. I've never really thought about it."

"Well think about it now. What will you do?"

Jenna curiously studied Dario. "Why are you so interested in that?"

He turned his head slightly until their eyes met. "I'm interested in everything about you."

There wasn't much she could say to that, and she knew exactly what he meant. She felt the same way about him. So, she thought about his question. "I think," she finally said, "that I want to have children of my own someday. And I think I could do that and maintain my career—but with the understanding that it will mean both my business and personal lives will suffer some."

"Why?"

"Because I won't be able to devote myself one hundred percent to either area of my life, will I? Until I started caring for Jamie, all of my efforts were directed toward the company. I worked twelve- and fourteen-hour days and loved every minute."

"And after Jamie?"

She turned in her seat again and smiled at the child. "After Jamie I cut my workdays nearly in half—except for the time immediately before the fashion shows. So what has happened is that I can't give my best effort to the business because of Jamie, but by the same token, I can't give my best effort to Jamie because of the business. There are going to be times while he's growing up that he's going to need me and I'm simply not going to be there for him, and all the so-called quality time at the end of my workday isn't going to change that one simple fact. Children's needs can't always wait until the end of the day when mom finally has time for them. If I ever have other children, that's something I'll have to consider very carefully."

"For someone who's never really thought about it, you've just given a very well-thought out answer."

She smiled tiredly. "I hope you took notes. I'm so weary right now I won't remember a single word of it by tomorrow."

"We're almost at the airport. You can sleep on the jet in a few minutes."

She rested the back of her head against her seat and stared out at the passing Illinois scenery, amazed at how calm she was. Perhaps it still hadn't hit her that she was really leaving.

Chapter Three

A hand gently touched her shoulder. "Jenna, we are in Lisbon. Wake up."

She blinked several times to clear away the cobwebs in front of her eyes and saw Dario leaning over her, Jamie in his arms. A slow, sleepy—and if she'd but known it, sexy—smile curved her mouth. "Hello."

"Boa noite," he said softly, his eyes warming her. "We have already cleared Customs. My car is waiting." He took her hand and pulled her to her feet, but instead of dropping it, he twined his fingers through hers as they climbed down the five steps from the small jet. He opened the rear door of a black four-door Mercedes and strapped Jamie into a babyseat; then he opened the front door for Jenna and politely held her elbow as she climbed in.

The sun hadn't set yet in the old city as Dario pulled the auto into the flow of traffic. And what traffic! She couldn't

44

believe the behavior of the other drivers as they neared the heart of Lisbon. For the first time, the word kamikaze had real meaning for her.

"I must stop at my attorney's office before we go to the Ribatejo," Dario explained.

"Ribatejo?"

"My home. *Our* home."

Jenna stared out the window at the passing scenery. Lisbon was undeniably beautiful. It was built on a series of steep, undulating hills, which carried rows of decorated houses on their sides. There were blocks of houses with beautiful wrought-iron balconies outside each of their windows. Their entire facades were covered with colored tiles.

There seemed to be a massive monument in every major square, with lesser monuments in lesser squares. She studied one in particular of a man on a horse with elaborate detailing as they were stopped at a red light. Dario noticed her interest. "No event in Portuguese history is left without its monument," he explained. "The fussier the better. I sometimes think my people love decoration simply for the sake of decoration."

Jenna smiled. "I like that. In fact, from what I've seen so far, I like Lisbon. There is an old-world charm here that's hard to find in the United States."

"In this area there certainly is."

"This area? Does it have a name?"

"The Alfama. It's the old Lisbon. The houses and narrow cobbled streets are hundreds of years old. But there are other parts, as in any large city, which are much less picturesque. We have had some political differences of opinion, as you will see in the grafitti covering the modern walls."

He parked in front of an office building and turned to her. "Will you two be all right waiting in the car?"

She couldn't help but smile at his concern. "We'll be fine, Dario."

Her eyes followed him until he disappeared into the building, then she leaned her head back against the car seat and studied her surroundings. The traffic held her in awe. She remembered reading somewhere that the natural courtesy of the Portuguese people disappeared when they were behind the wheel of a car, but she would never have believed it was this bad. They seemed to look upon pedestrians as their natural enemy.

Dario returned a few minutes later and tossed a file he had picked up from his attorney into the back seat. He pulled into the flow of traffic again, but not without a fight. Cars came out of nowhere, horns blasting, startling Jenna until she was sure there wasn't a gasp left in her. She was holding the edge of her seat so tightly her knuckles were white.

Dario missed very little where she was concerned. "If you are going to be here for any length of time you will have to get used to this."

"I think I'll let you drive." A horn blasted from the car next to her and she jumped. "Don't you people have any rules of the road?"

"Two major ones," he said dryly. "The first is that one car should never let another pass without a fight."

"Something tells me I'm not going to find much comfort in rule number two."

"The second," he smiled, "is that there is no such thing as the wrong side of the road."

"I was right. No comfort at all. But at least," she conceded, "you seem more sane than your countrymen."

They stopped at a red light and for reasons known only to themselves, people in the cars ahead, behind and next to them, began honking impatiently. It was deafening. "How do people ever sleep at night with all this noise?" she yelled across to Dario.

"There is a law prohibiting the sounding of horns at night within the city limits. And only parking lights may be used after dark."

A sudden vision of all those drivers with no horns through which to vent their frustrations caused her to grin widely. "That must make them crazy!"

His eyes creased at the corners. "They can still get their point across. Most European cars have something called a flicker switch. The result is that one drives around with flashing fireflies on every hand."

Jenna laughed—a lovely, infectious sound that delighted Dario.

The Mercedes crossed an enormous red bridge over a fast-flowing river. "Below us is the Tagus, pronounced *Tah-goosh*," he explained to his interested passenger. "It is from that river, only further north, that Columbus set sail for America. The Ribatejo runs along its banks with its pastures of fighting bulls and horses."

"Fighting bulls? As in bullfight?" she asked distastefully.

He nodded. "Our ranch is located between Santarem, the capital of the Ribatejo, and the Vila Franca de Xira. We will be there shortly."

But her mind was still on what he'd said before. In all the conversations they'd had three years ago, she'd never asked him what he did for a living. "Are you saying that you raise fighting bulls?"

He glanced over at her. "And horses. Why do you ask like that?"

"Like what?"

"Like you've just discovered I'm a war criminal."

A chagrined smile touched her mouth. "I didn't mean for it to come out like that. It's just that the thought of raising those poor creatures just so they can be slaughtered in a fight upsets me."

A corner of his mouth lifted. "You have quite an education ahead of you, Jenna Hart. Those 'poor creatures' as you so inappropriately call them, weigh thousands of pounds. They're big and they're vicious, and they'd just as soon kill a man as look at him. And as you will see, in a Portuguese bullfight, the bull is never killed."

"What about the horses? I've seen films of Spanish bullfights, and the horses are battered to death by the bull."

"Again, I say to you that this is Portugal. We do things differently. Our horses, as you will see, are thoroughbreds. They play an important part in a Portuguese bullfight, but they are *never* touched by the bull. For a rider to allow his horse to even be grazed by a bull is a disgrace."

She still wasn't convinced, but dropped the subject until she'd done some reading of her own. She gazed at the passing scenery again. The land was flat and lusty, but the sun was setting and it was difficult to see things clearly. At one point they encountered on the road several oxen whose horns, to Jenna at least, seemed to have a fifteen-foot spread from point to point. Dario drove the car onto the grassy roadside and passed them easily.

Jenna turned to check on Jamie. He was just beginning to nod off. She relaxed back in her seat and studied the carved profile of the man next to her. "Do you honestly think what we're doing is going to work?" she suddenly asked.

Dario met her look. "This is a strange time to be asking me that."

"Perhaps," she agreed, "but I'm still asking. Do you?"

He pulled the car onto the side of the road and turned toward her, his arm over the back of her seat. "I don't know, Jenna. Any more than you do. I can foresee clashes between us on the proper way to raise Jamie, and that is as it should be."

"And in those clashes, which of us will get his way?"

A corner of his mouth lifted. "Whoever yells the loudest."

"I don't yell."

"Oh, something tells me you will if you get mad enough. You and I are not unalike, you know." He absently lifted some strands of her silky hair and let it fall through his fingers. "We both have strong wills. We'll have our share of arguments, but that's what this is all about, isn't it? So that we'll both contribute to his life in a way we couldn't do if we lived apart. If we're going to agree on everything, you might as well have stayed in Chicago."

"I suppose so." Her eyes met his. "I have to admit that I'm a little frightened, though. I don't think it's really hit me yet that I'm going to be living in a foreign country, in a home I've never seen and with people I've never met. I don't even speak the language."

"Soon you'll see the home and meet the people. You can learn the language. And I'll be there for you if you need me."

The touch of his fingers lightly brushing her neck as he toyed with her hair sent a wave of awareness down her spine.

Dario turned and started the car again. They were silent for the rest of the journey, each wrapped up in individual thoughts. The car passed through a wrought-iron gate in a formidable rose-colored stone wall and traveled down a sandy drive leading past walled-in pastures. They stopped in front of an imposing rose-colored villa. Lights blazed warmly inside and out.

"My home," Dario told her. "Welcome."

Still staring in something akin to wonder at the most beautiful home she had ever seen, she managed to breathe, "Thank you."

A small, wizened man came running down the steps of the villa. "Senhor! Welcome home."

"*Obrigado*, Tomaso. I would like to present Miss Hart." He turned to Jenna. "This is Tomaso. He has been with the Montoya family since I was a child."

Jenna smiled at the little, walnut colored man, who bowed crisply from the waist in a show of old-fashioned gallantry which warmed her. "I'm pleased to meet you," she acknowledged.

Now it was his turn to smile. "*Muito Obrigado*." He turned to his boss for instructions, which Dario gave in Portuguese.

While Tomaso busied himself carrying in the luggage, Dario helped Jenna climb out of the car, then lifted a sleeping Jamie from his comfortable babyseat and gently held him in his arms. The more Jenna saw the two of them together, the more she realized what a terrible mistake she had made in not telling Dario about Jamie's existence in the first place.

As they walked up the steps and through the huge carved oak doors leading into the villa, a lovely dark-haired woman whom Jenna judged to be about her own age, ran up to them, excitedly rattling off a rapid spate of Portuguese, none of which Jenna could follow.

"Speak English, Isabella," Dario admonished affectionately, "so our guest can understand you. This," he explained to Jenna, "is my sister, Isabella."

The Portuguese woman's brown eyes sparkled as she held out her hand to Jenna. "I am so pleased to meet you at last!" Then she moved beside her brother so she could see the face of the sleeping baby. "Oh," she melted, "so this is my nephew. He looks so much like Carlos." She turned to Jenna. "Grandmama will be thrilled to see him. She still misses Carlos sorely. This little fellow will give her something to get up for in the mornings."

Jenna's guilt returned twofold.

"Which room have you prepared for her?" Dario interrupted. "It was a long trip. I am sure she would like to freshen up."

"Of course." Isabella looped her arm through Jenna's in a friendly fashion. "You have the tapestry room," she explained as they walked up the curved staircase which was carpeted in a rich, red wine plush, perfect with the dark wood of the railing and foyer floor and paneled walls.

Dario followed close behind. "Will Jamie be in my room?" Jenna asked, looking back at him.

"He will be in the nursery with his nurse."

She stopped walking and turned to face him, not at all pleased. "I thought I was here to help take care of him?"

"You are here to help *raise* him. For his day-to-day care we have hired a woman trained to do just that."

"But Jamie is used to me," she protested.

"And now he will get used to Maria," Dario informed her, calmly walking past her on the steps and down the long hallway as Jenna stood helplessly by and watched. One minute they were rationally discussing whether or not the situation would work, and the next, he was *telling* her what he intended for Jamie as though she had no say whatsoever. "Oh!" she finally managed.

Isabella touched Jenna's arm sympathetically. "Come. I will show you your room. You can have it out with him later. I will even help," she offered, taking her arm again.

The bedroom was nearly as big as Jenna's entire apartment. Two rich-looking Oriental rugs lay atop the highly polished wood floor, one next to the high double bed and the other in front of the floor-to-ceiling windows at the other end of the room. The walls were rose hued, the ceiling white and against one wall was a long carved rosewood dresser with a gilded wood mirror running its length.

Jenna looked around with appreciative hazel eyes. "It's enchanting!"

"This is my favorite guest bedroom," Isabella admitted. "Grandmother and I thought you would like it." She patted out a wrinkle in the rose-colored bedspread, then smiled across the room at Jenna. "We are having some guests for dinner this evening—a few friends and neighbors. If you would care to join us, we would be delighted."

"Perhaps for a few minutes, after I've showered and changed. But I think I'll skip dinner, if you don't mind. I'm not very hungry."

"Of course. I understand completely. I, myself, am never hungry after a long flight. It does something to the appetite." She looked thoughtfully around the room, wondering if she had forgotten to tell her guest anything. "Oh, yes. Your bath is behind that door. Tomaso should already have brought your luggage up . . ." She spotted it in a corner. "Ah, there it is. If you need anything, simply pull that tapestry cord next to your bed and someone will be up."

Jenna walked over to the bed and studied the beautifully needlepointed bell pull. She had never seen one before.

"Medieval, *noa?*" Isabella asked. "You will find that the Montoya family is very traditional." She glanced at her watch. "I must be getting back to the guests. When you are ready, simply follow the long downstairs hall to the fourth door. That will be the salon where everyone is."

"I will, thank you, Isabella."

The Portuguese woman kissed her cheek. "You are most welcome."

When she had gone, Jenna looked around the room again before digging into her luggage and unpacking. When that was done, she showered and changed into a sherbet orange dress with a tailored top and stand-up collar and a full skirt that was belted at her slender waist. She brushed her hair until it fell to her shoulders in shining waves and then looked at herself in the large mirror. The woman who looked back at her didn't seem to be the same one who had left Chicago such a short time ago. The dark-lashed eyes were more luminous, the mouth more vulnerable. The reflection made her uncomfortable and she looked away.

She left her room intent on seeing Jamie. Dario had

gone down the long hall with him so, she reasoned, the nursery must be there somewhere.

Halfway down she began lightly tapping on doors and opening them to see if Jamie was there. She tapped on the third door and no one answered, so she opened it and stepped partially into the room. It was even larger than hers and very much a man's room, with its rich, masculine colors and ebony furniture. This certainly wasn't Jamie's room. Dario suddenly stepped out of a door, obviously fresh from his shower. His black hair was damp and unruly, as though he had just rubbed it with a towel. His bronzed, powerful body was covered only by a towel around his waist and one thrown across the back of his neck. Jenna was caught completely off-guard. She had tried to imagine what he would look like, and now here he was. Short black hairs curled on his muscular chest, forming a "T," the stem of which disappeared under his towel. She was completely unconscious of the very thorough once-over she was giving him until her eyes met his amused tawny ones.

"Like what you see?" he asked.

Her cheeks grew pink, but she held his gaze firmly with her own. "Actually, yes. I do."

He moved closer to her and ran the back of his hand down her warm cheek. "Bold words for such pink cheeks."

She could actually feel her heart pumping. Her foot twitched at the temptation to step away from him, but she forced herself to stay still. She wasn't some silly schoolgirl. Jenna cleared her throat. "I was looking for Jamie's room. I want to meet this nurse you seem so pleased with."

Dario placed his finger under her chin and looked steadily into her eyes. "Stop talking."

Her unsure eyes searched his. "I don't think I can. I always talk too much when I'm nervous."

"I make you nervous?"

"Extremely."

He moved his mouth closer to hers. "Shhhhhhh."

"Dario . . ."

He kissed first one side of her mouth and then the other with a slow deliberateness that had her heart pounding so hard she was sure he could hear it.

Her eyelids drifted closed, but opened as he lightly touched his mouth to hers in short, gentle kisses. His hands cupped her face and he looked deeply into her eyes. "I've wanted to do that ever since I saw you standing so nervously in the airport, waiting for me."

There was a sharp knock on the door. Jenna jumped and put her hand over her heart.

"Who is it?" Dario asked impatiently, his eyes still on Jenna.

"Tomaso."

"*Momento.*" The man and woman studied each other quietly.

"I wish you hadn't done that," Jenna finally told him. "I think we need to keep some distance between us if we're going to be living in the same house. Anything else would be improper, don't you agree?"

"Improper for whom?"

Before she could answer, Tomaso knocked again. Dario moved to the door and put his hand on the knob. "I'd like to finish this conversation some time," he informed her, pulling it open.

"I'm sure we will," she said as she walked past him and Tomaso, whose eyes followed her curiously.

"Jamie is at the end of the hall," Dario called after her.

Jenna walked quickly without looking back. When she got to the right door, she paused before it and took a deep breath, her eyes closed. Oh, she *was* attracted to him. Far too much for her own peace of mind, under the circumstances.

She pushed the door open. A nurse was sitting in an easy chair near a light, reading a book. Jenna forced Dario from her mind and managed a smile. The woman was round and motherly. She smiled back at Jenna as she put the book on a table and walked over to her. "You are the child's aunt?"

She nodded. "How is he?"

"Fine, *Menina.*" Her English was heavily accented and difficult to understand. "He is a perfect . . ."

"Angel?" Jenna finished for her.

"Exactly! Come. See." She led Jenna to one of the cosiest cribs she had ever seen. Jamie was sound asleep in the middle of a dozen stuffed animals, some new, some of which had obviously been favorites of other children in years gone by. "He looks happy, *noa?*" Maria whispered.

Jenna smiled softly as she pushed a dark curl off his forehead. "He looks happy, yes," she agreed. "Will you be staying with him all night?"

The middle-aged woman nodded her dark head. "*Sim.* I sleep on a bed over there." She pointed to a comfortable looking daybed. "And when he is a little older I will sleep in the room attached to the nursery."

But Jenna still looked worried.

Maria touched her shoulder reassuringly. "Truly, I am

good with babies. I will love him as my own. Do not worry.''

A corner of Jenna's mouth lifted. "Thank you, Maria. I can see that.''

She bobbed her head. *"Nao ha de que.* Welcome.''

Jenna closed the door quietly behind her and headed down the hall, her mind at ease—about Jamie, at least. When she got to Dario's door, she unconsciously paused and then moved on, only to find Dario himself standing at the top of the stairs, one broad shoulder leaning against the wall. "You really should learn to disguise the expression in those beautiful eyes of yours. They give so much away.''

Jenna stopped a few feet away. Dario had changed into a V-necked white sweater with the sleeves pushed halfway up his muscular forearms, and navy blue trousers. His thick hair was still damp, but combed now. One side of his mouth curved in a lazy smile. She ignored his remark. "Are you waiting for me?''

"Yes. We have dinner guests this evening. I will escort you.''

She smiled politely as she walked past him. "That isn't necessary. Isabella told me which room they're in. I can find it myself.''

Dario caught her arm in a firm but gentle grip, hauling her up short. "You are a guest in my home, and as such you will not go to a dinner party here, or anywhere else, unescorted.''

Jenna looked from the hand on her arm to the face of the man holding it. "That's archaic.''

"Perhaps. But it is the Portuguese way.''

They fell into step, passing by oil portraits, some of great age, hanging on the richly paneled walls.

"My ancestors," Dario answered her unasked question. "Some of them are quite interesting. I will tell you about them sometime."

At the bottom of the stairs they turned right, but before they had gone ten steps, a voice stopped them. "Dario!"

The man smiled as a woman of astonishing beauty approached and put her hands into his. "Ines, what a pleasant surprise. I thought you were still in France."

She smiled into his eyes. "I decided to come home for awhile."

Jenna, seemingly forgotten, cleared her throat. Dario remembered his manners. "Jenna Hart, I would like you to meet Ines de Santos. Ines was Elisa's sister. In America I believe you would call her my sister-in-law."

Ines extended a soft, long-fingered hand. "I understand from Isabella that you will be staying for a time with little Jamie."

"That's right." She felt Dario's eyes narrow on her.

"There you two are!" Isabella walked toward them and proprietarily took one of Jenna's arms. "Come, Jenna. You must meet the rest of the guests." Dario followed with Ines.

There were several people in the main salon. It was a large room, as all the rooms in the villa apparently were. But even so, it managed to be friendly. There was an area at the center which was perfect for conversation. Matching overstuffed leather couches, each of them a good eight feet long, faced each other. Between them sat a large, square coffee table, beautifully inlaid. One wall was dominated by a fireplace, another by several glass-paned doors, all of which opened into a magnificent garden.

A young man whose brown eyes had lit up appreciatively at the sight of her walked up to Jenna and extended his hand. Without taking his eyes from her, he spoke to Isabella. "Come, Bella, introduce me to this beautiful American girl."

Isabella shook her dark head and smiled. "You will have to forgive Basilio," she told Jenna in an aside which the young man was obviously meant to hear. "He has absolutely no manners and even less common sense."

It washed right over him. "Well, Bella, if you won't do the honors, I shall introduce myself." He bowed gallantly. "I am Basilio de Santos, brother of Ines. We live on an adjoining ranch a few miles away."

Jenna liked his unaffected charm. She gave him a graceful curtsey. "I'm Jenna Hart."

"Ah," he sighed theatrically, placing his hand over his heart. "How appropriate that you should have that name, for you have surely stolen mine."

Jenna's lovely laugh drifted through the room.

Basilio winced in mock pain. "She strikes me to the quick!" Then he looked over at Dario, who appeared singularly unamused at his neighbor's antics. "I must say, my friend, you have confirmed my belief in your good taste—not to mention luck, in women."

Ines interrupted. "My understanding is that Miss Hart came with the child. It was hardly Dario's choice."

Basilio raised an expressive brow. "Dario always has a choice, my sister."

Isabella poked the young man in the ribs with her elbow and frowned meaningfully.

Dario's tawny eyes half smiled into Jenna's. "I see you will be well taken care of. Excuse me, please." He walked off with Ines, while Jenna tried hard not to watch them.

Isabella took her arm again. "Come. I wish you to meet my grandmother."

Basilio took her other arm. "I will lend you moral support."

"More like *im*moral support, if I know you, Basilio de Santos," Isabella snapped at him, much as a sister would to a brother.

"Ah, Bella, you know me too, too well."

Isabella looked at Jenna and shook her head. "He is outrageous, but hard as it is for you to believe now, you will get used to him."

He grinned unrepentantly at both of them. "I certainly hope so. Starting with tomorrow night. How about a date, Jenna Hart?"

A dimple appeared near the corner of Jenna's mouth. "You don't waste any time, do you?"

He wiggled his eyebrows.

"Why don't you just go away?" Isabella grumbled in exasperation, pulling on Jenna's arm and leading her to Senhora Montoya, who was sitting quietly. The old woman, her skin like fragile parchment, was dressed from head to toe in black, with a weblike black lace shawl over her thin shoulders. Her brown eyes were clear and sharp and they looked Jenna over thoroughly. Jenna unconsciously straightened her shoulders and met that look.

"Grandmama," Isabella introduced, "this is Jamie's aunt, Jenna Hart." And with those words, Isabella left them alone.

Jenna felt uneasy and terribly guilty, but none of this was visible on her composed face. The old woman suddenly spoke. "Come child. Pull up the ottoman. We have much to speak of."

As Jenna obeyed, her eyes instinctively searched the

room for Dario. She found him, listening attentively to what another man was saying. But then, as though he felt her need for reassurance, he looked up and straight into her eyes. In those seconds, for Jenna, at least, no one else in the room existed. Only Dario.

Someone walked between them and she blinked. The spell was broken.

Taking a much needed breath, she remembered the Senhora and turned back to her. "Excuse me, please. My . . . mind wandered."

The old woman missed little. The look that had passed between her grandson and this woman had spoken volumes—and it hadn't pleased her. "I wish you to tell me of my great-grandson. Is he a fine, strong boy like his father?"

"He is."

"And his coloring? Dark or light?"

"So far Jamie seems to be taking his coloring from Carlos."

"Ah," she sighed in satisfaction, sitting back in her chair, her long fingered hands folded in her lap. "That is good. He will be a Montoya."

Jenna couldn't help the smile which tugged at her mouth. "No matter what his coloring, Senhora, he is a Montoya."

The old woman nodded, her piercing eyes on the girl. "You were not going to tell us about him."

It was difficult, but Jenna was straightforward. "That's right. I wasn't."

"At least you are honest. Would you ever have if Dario hadn't found out?"

Jenna lifted her shoulders. "I don't know. Certainly not until he was much older. My sister wanted me to take care of her son, and I knew your family could take him away from me. No matter how sorry I felt for you over your loss, I couldn't risk that.''

The old woman leaned forward and squeezed her hand, a warm light entering her eyes at this surprising American's candid responses. "I understand." She leaned back in her chair again. "So, tell me of your sister. What manner of person was she?"

Jenna smiled sadly. After all this time, she still missed her. "She was lovely, gentle, kind—and very much in love with her husband.''

"I should hope so, after the disgrace she heaped upon the name of Montoya.''

Jenna blinked at the unexpectedness of the words. "Caroline never disgraced anyone, Senhora," she responded with more calm than she felt. She started to say something about Carlos' lack of honesty, but refrained. The last thing she wanted to do was get into a name-calling match with Jamie's great-grandmother.

The old woman stared into space for a moment before her gaze returned to Jenna. "Were they happy, Carlos and your sister?"

"Very."

"Dario said so also, but I am glad to hear it from you." Her eyes grew sad as they rested on her grandson. "I am beginning to wonder if there are such things as happy endings anymore.''

Dario chose that moment to move behind his grandmother's chair and placed his hands on her frail shoulders. "Are you ready for dinner?"

The old woman patted his bronzed hand and nodded. "Yes. I grow tired talking, even to this most charming girl.''

A look of complete understanding passed between the two of them. The family ties here were strong and Jenna was reminded with a pang just how much an outsider she was.

"Come, Jenna Hart," the old woman invited as she rose. "You will join us."

Jenna smiled and rose also. "Thank you, but no. I'm too tired to eat. I think I'll just get a book and retire to my room, if you don't mind." Her eyes met Dario's. "May I get one from your study?"

His eyes rested on her. "Yes. It's next to this room."

When everyone had gone, she walked into his study and glanced over the bookshelves built into the dark walls. There were books in Portuguese, French and English, but nothing that she really wanted to read.

With a little sigh, she strolled over to the open door leading out to the courtyard and breathed deeply of the fresh air. She didn't see Dario enter the room and then stand quietly watching her with enigmatic tawny eyes.

But she felt his presence.

She didn't see him turn and, leaving, close the door silently behind him.

But she knew when he'd gone.

Her body relaxed. She leaned against the doorframe, her arms folded under her breasts. This was quite a revelation for her. Never in her life had she been so aware of a man. It was a little frightening.

But it was also strangely exciting.

Chapter Four

When Jenna awoke the next morning, she walked over to her open windows and sat in the window seat hugging her knees, breathing deeply of the citrus-scented air. Her room was directly over the gardens and the view was wonderful. In the distance were rolling, walled-in pastures and picturesque white stables in the Spanish tradition. This was so different from what she was used to. Already she felt as though a whole new dimension had been added to her life.

And then there was Dario Montoya. She couldn't stop thinking about him.

Shaking her head, she rose and stretched. It was still early. She wanted to get started on her first day in Portugal. Her natural curiosity was already urging her to explore. And she was also aware of a certain responsibility. Half of the ranch belonged to Jamie, and she had to take an interest in it and learn what she could about what went on there.

She showered and then dressed in a pair of white, slim-fitting jeans and an apple green outsize blouse which she belted with a low-riding sash. Thinking more of comfort than fashion, she brushed her blonde hair into a ponytail and tied it with a green ribbon.

With a lilt in her step, she walked down the long hall, surreptitiously eyeing Dario's room in passing. As she neared Jamie's room, she pushed all thought of Dario from her mind in order to concentrate on the child. This was her time with Jamie and not anything or anyone was going to intrude. Jenna pushed Jamie's door open and started to walk in, but stopped suddenly at the sight of the baby sitting on his great-grandmother's lap, smiling from ear to ear as the old woman cooed at him in Portuguese, her eyes damp with emotion. Jenna's throat constricted. If she had ever questioned the rightness of bringing Jamie here, the questions were gone. This was the way it should be.

Jenna felt a presence behind her and inhaled the clean scent of a man's aftershave. "Now," a deep voice asked softly just above her ear, "aren't you glad that I persuaded you to bring Jamie here?"

Her betraying heart skipped a beat. She looked over her shoulder at him, one shapely brow lifted. "Persuaded?" she asked dryly. "Somehow the word 'bulldozed' pops into my mind."

His tawny eyes smiled into hers before turning their attention to the scene in the room. After a moment he placed his hand under her elbow and turned her around. "Let's leave them to get to know one another. I'll show you where we usually eat breakfast."

By the time they got there, she was glad he had. It was at the other end of the villa and outside. She would never have found it alone. It was worth the walk, though. The lovely loggia looked out over a pool and manicured green lawn. In the distance were the white stables with arched doorways she had seen from her bedroom window.

Jenna sat down with a contented sigh. "Do you always breakfast out-of-doors like this?"

Dario sat down across from her. "Whenever weather permits."

"A perfect way to start the day."

She eyed the food on the table. "What are you having?"

"I have already eaten, but I'll have some coffee with you."

Jenna laid a linen napkin on her lap and smoothed out nonexistent wrinkles, suddenly self-conscious with this man. "If you have other things to do, there's no need for you to sit here . . ."

His eyes rested on her for a long moment. "I know." He poured her a cup of coffee, then another for himself.

She helped herself to a croissant, still miraculously warm, and some honey. "Have you been up long?" she asked, biting into the flaky pastry.

"Days begin early here."

"What do you do?"

He shrugged his wide shoulders. "On a ranch this size, there is always something to do. Bulls need testing. Horses need training. Breeders must be selected and made use of during the appropriate times."

She took another bite of croissant and savored it for a moment before continuing the conversation. "I'd like to hear some more about Portuguese bullfighting. Exactly how is it different from Spanish bullfighting.''

He leaned back in his chair and steepled his fingers under his chin, studying her with warm eyes. ''Are you truly interested, or simply making conversation?''

A smile tugged at her mouth. ''A little of both, I suppose.''

He raised his coffee cup to her. ''Marks for honesty. The answer to your question is that the Spaniards do most of their fighting on foot, and kill the bull after the fight in the ring in front of the spectators. The Portuguese fight the bull from horseback and on foot, and the bull is never killed in the ring.''

She eyed him with interest. There was something in his voice which caught her attention. ''You're a bullfighter, aren't you?'' she finally asked, already knowing the answer.

''Dario is one of the best in Portugal.'' Ines walked up the steps, dressed in a stunning riding outfit that showed off her voluptuous figure to great advantage, and kissed him on the cheek. ''I hope you don't mind my coming over so early, but I thought perhaps we could ride out together.'' She sat down and poured herself some coffee. ''There are some things I need to talk to you about. Basilio is thinking about purchasing a breeding bull from the Duarte Ranch. Personally, I think it would be an expensive mistake.''

He inclined his dark head. ''Certainly.'' He looked back at Jenna. ''What are you going to do with your day?''

She leaned back in her chair and gracefully stretched her arms over her head. ''The weather is so beautiful. I thought I might take a walk. Spend some time with Jamie.

Other than that," she lifted her shoulders, "I don't know."

"I would prefer that you don't walk alone."

His protectiveness was obvious—and she found she rather liked it after all the years of watching out for herself. "I won't get lost, if that's what you're worried about. You're talking to a woman who found her way back to her room last night, completely unassisted."

His half smile warmed her. "It isn't that. You don't know the ranch yet, or where it's safe to walk."

"I concede the point. Perhaps you could tell me where *not* to go and everyone will be happy?"

The grooves in his cheeks deepened more. He wasn't used to having his "suggestions" questioned like this, but from her, he didn't mind. "You are a very determined girl."

"Woman," she corrected.

At that, he laughed. "I knew I was in trouble the moment the word left my lips."

"Well," she challenged, "wouldn't you object to being called a boy?"

"At thirty-two, I expect I would."

She eyed him curiously. "How old were you when you first considered yourself a man?" She intended it as an innocent enough question, remembering how she had really considered herself a woman when she turned eighteen.

Dario playfully tweaked her straight nose. Ines watched all this with interested eyes, looking from Jenna to Dario and back again. "When I was thirteen," he answered.

It took a moment, but his meaning finally dawned on her. Jenna's mouth curved as she slowly shook her head. "I walked right into that one, didn't I?"

Before he could answer, a man came to the table and spoke rapidly in Portuguese to Dario, who listened intently then rose to leave. "I will meet you by the stables, Ines, in about half an hour. In the meantime, you know the ranch as well as anyone. Please explain to Jenna where she may and may not go. And in particular about Morte Negro." With a slight bow and a last look at Jenna, Dario strode across the lawn. Jenna watched until he disappeared from sight. Ines cleared her throat and Jenna jumped. She had completely forgotten about the other woman. "Can I pour you some coffee?"

Ines pointed at her half-full cup. "I have some, thank you."

Jenna searched her mind for something they could talk about, then she hit upon Dario's parting words. "What is Morte Negro?"

Ines sipped her coffee, studying Jenna over the rim of her cup. "Morte Negro, or Black Death, as he would be called in English, is the name of a bull. He is so vicious that he has been separated from the rest of the bulls to graze alone."

Jenna shivered involuntarily. "Why is he kept here at all? Shouldn't he be destroyed before someone gets hurt?"

Ines was appalled by her ignorance. "Destroyed? That animal is worth a fortune for breeding alone."

"I can see I have a lot to learn about the bullfighting business."

"You certainly do. You're in the very heart of Portuguese bull breeding country."

"Where is this Morte Negro, anyway? I'd like to steer clear of him—no pun intended."

Ines smiled. "Steer clear. Very good. Do you see the area behind me?"

"The stables?"

"*Sim*. But beyond that are the pastures, most of them divided by stone walls. Morte Negro is in one of those."

"And the other bulls?" She didn't relish the thought of unexpectedly meeting them either.

"They are in that direction also, but in different pastures."

"So that area is to be avoided," Jenna confirmed. "Where will I be safe walking?"

Ines pointed. "If you follow the sand track out the other way you will find only the horses." She delicately sipped her coffee. "Tell me . . . may I call you Jenna?"

"Please."

"Thank you. And you may call me Ines. Tell me, Jenna, do you ride at all?"

"Yes. I had a friend in high school who had horses and used to take me riding with her. I'm afraid my form is less than textbook, but I can at least stay in the saddle."

Ines clicked her tongue. "Perhaps a few lessons would do the job. You should know how to ride properly. Particularly here on the ranch. Horses are our means of transportation more times than not."

Jenna studied the other woman curiously.

Ines frowned at her. "What is it? Is my lipstick smeared?" she asked worriedly.

Jenna smiled. "No. Your lipstick is perfect. I'm just having trouble adjusting to the way you're behaving today. I expected you to be . . . different."

Ines tilted her head. "Different, how?"

Jenna studied her. "It's hard to explain." She leaned forward, her elbows on the table. "Last night you seemed hostile toward me. Today you're not at all. Will the real Ines please stand up?''

Ines laughed. ''Oh, that! I was just in a bad mood last night. You will discover, as I am afraid everyone else has, that I am a moody woman. There will be days when you love to be around me and days when you'll groan at the mere mention of my name.''

Jenna smiled, relieved. ''To be honest, I thought it had something to do with Dario.''

''Jealousy?''

''Something like that—though even if it were, you have nothing to worry about. You know the reason I'm here, and it isn't Dario.''

Ines lifted her hand dismissingly. ''Even if it were it wouldn't matter. I'd be lying if I told you I wouldn't throw myself at the man's feet if he wanted me, but he doesn't. At least not for anything beyond friendship.''

Ines glanced at her elegant watch and got to her feet. ''I must be going now or I'll miss Dario.'' She held out her hand to Jenna. ''I hope we have a chance to get to know one another better before I leave for France. Enjoy your walk!'' she called over her shoulder as she headed for the stables.

Still smiling, Jenna pushed her chair back and started down the sandy track she found just around the side of the house and past a walled-in pasture. She breathed deeply of the heady scent of orange blossoms and enjoyed the feel of the warm sun.

She willed all thoughts from her head except those directly concerned with her surroundings.

With no little effort, she climbed to the top of the six-foot stone wall and straddled the top, her hand shading her eyes from the sun as she looked for the horses Ines said she would find. There was nothing there but some trees, lots of grass and wildflowers. She jumped down from the wall and picked herself a bouquet, which she carried along with her, sniffing it, as she walked through the pasture.

She completely lost track of time, savoring her freedom. Jamie was going to love it here. Another point to Dario.

She bent over to pick another flower when a noise to her left startled her. Turning quickly, she found two hot black eyes staring at her out of one of the most horrible faces she had ever seen. A bull! But Ines had said that only horses were in this particular pasture! The creature couldn't have been more than ten yards away. The great lump of muscle on its back was raised. His hooves pawed the earth menacingly and his curving, needle-sharp horns sliced the air.

Her heart stopped, and then started pounding furiously. More than anything in the world at that moment she wanted to run. But her instincts told her to stand absolutely still. She was barely breathing, and her eyes were fixed on the great hulking animal, whose eyes were in turn fixed steadily upon her. One move, one blink of an eye and it was all over.

She knew without question that this was Morte Negro.

How long the two stood like that, she had no idea, but it seemed an eternity. Her muscles ached with the strain of remaining motionless. The bull hadn't moved either, but simply stood there watching. He obviously didn't know what to make of her. Jenna knew from a television program that bulls had terrible eyesight. For all Morte Negro knew, she was a tree, but one deep breath and he would attack—and she had no place to go. Her fingers were numb from gripping her now wilted bouquet. Her heart pounded so hard she was sure he could see the movement through her blouse.

Suddenly the voice she most longed to hear called from behind the bull. "Jenna!"

She had been concentrating so hard on Morte Negro that she hadn't even noticed Dario's approach. Likewise, the bull had been so intent on watching her that he hadn't noticed Dario until he spoke. Then the animal wheeled to face him. Jenna allowed herself the luxury of closing her eyes. The air left her lungs in a relieved rush. Dario was here. Everything would be all right.

"Do exactly as I tell you," Dario said. "Run as quickly as you can toward the wall."

She wanted desperately to ask him what he was going to do, but didn't dare for fear of attracting Morte Negro's attention.

"Don't stop for anything. Do you understand?"

"Yes."

"All right. Now!" Dario and the horse moved, and the bull charged them. Jenna took off, running literally for her life. She made it halfway to the wall, but suddenly her foot hit a hole and she crashed to the ground. Swearing softly, she got up, but her ankle was injured and gave out under her weight. The bull was confused now. He didn't know whom to attack. The dark man on the horse or the thing on the ground which had proven itself not to be a tree after all, just as he had suspected.

Dario leaned forward in the saddle and taunted the bull to get his attention away from the injured woman. *"Hoi! Toiro!* Come pick on someone your own size, my friend."

Jenna's heart lurched when the bull took the bait and attacked. Man and horse maneuvered out of reach of the killer horns by inches. Her breath caught in her throat as the bull circled with astonishing quickness and attacked again and again, each time striking so close that, from where Jenna sat, she couldn't tell whether they made contact or not. Dario's carved face was a study in concentration as he tried to predict each of the bull's moves. One mistake and man and horse would both be killed.

After the next charge, the bull stopped in a flurry of hooves and dust to study his opponents and assess the situation. Dario, his eyes never leaving the beast, called to Jenna. "You are hurt?"

"My ankle."

"Can you stand?"

"On one foot."

"Do it!"

"But . . ."

"For God's sake, don't argue with me, woman!"

She stood, balancing on one foot. The bull chose that moment to charge and again missed the horse by only inches. While the bull was turning to attack once more, Dario and his horse continued on toward Jenna at a remarkable speed, barely slowing at all as they neared her. Dario reached down with one powerful arm as they flashed by and scooped her up and onto the saddle in front of him. They approached the wall at full tilt, the bull following closely behind.

Horse, man and woman flew to safety over the wall. Dario stopped suddenly and wheeled the horse around, then sat silently in the saddle staring at the wall. Jenna would discover later that angry bulls were known to leap over six-foot walls with relative ease. Fortunately, she then sat in ignorance.

Dario held her tightly against his chest as he rode over to a shady tree. After dismounting, he lifted Jenna off the black stallion's back and laid her on the grass. Wordlessly he probed her ankle with his strong but gentle fingers until she winced. He sat back on his heels and dragged his hand through his thick hair. His unsmiling eyes held hers. "It's sprained."

She raised herself on her elbows. "Are you sure it isn't broken?"

"I'm sure, though it probably feels like it. Sprains can be as painful."

"How did you happen to find me?"

His eyes grew darker as they rested on her. "Luck," he said tightly. "Ines mentioned that she had told you where you could walk and I realized she wasn't aware that we had changed Morte Negro's pasture. She thought the horses were still out here." There was a long pause. "I had no idea what I would find when I finally arrived."

Jenna raised a trembling hand to push the hair off her forehead. "Neither did I. I don't think I've ever been so frightened in my life."

Dario cupped her cheek in his hand. "Nor have I." There was an intensity in his voice which silenced Jenna. She swallowed and lowered her eyes.

Dario gazed at her softly parted mouth, then slowly rubbed his thumb against it. Jenna raised her eyes to his and started to speak, but his thumb pressed against her lips to silence her. He forced his eyes from hers as he took off his shirt and ripped it into several ribbons which he carefully bound around her ankle. She had to bite her lip to keep from gasping at the pain. To take her mind off it, she looked at Dario. His dark head was bent over her leg. His strong shoulders and muscular torso seemed to have been sculpted by a master. Jenna found herself imagining how his smooth skin would feel under her fingertips and mentally ran them over his chest.

With a sigh, she raised her eyes to his face only to find an amused Dario watching her. Her cheeks flushed delicately, but she held his gaze. He took her hands and placed them on his chest, and then, holding her wrists, slowly slid her hands down his chest to the hard wall of his stomach.

Jenna swallowed.

"You should learn to veil those wonderful eyes of yours," he told her. "Every thought is there for the world to read."

"I'll remember that in the future." The warmth of his tanned skin under her hands was creating a slow, responding warmth deep in her. "I hope you aren't expecting me to reciprocate," she finally managed in a light tone, referring to what he had just done with her hands.

"Not yet."

Jenna, who rarely had trouble meeting anyone's eyes, had to look down. "Perhaps we should be getting back to the house."

"Don't be afraid of me, Jenna."

"It's not you I'm afraid of," she said quietly. "It's me."

"Why?"

She lifted her slender shoulders. "I don't really know, Dario. Perhaps I find myself more attracted to you than I want to be."

A corner of his mouth lifted. "You are one of the most honest people I've ever met, Jenna. I noticed that the first time we met. It's one of the reasons I've found you so . . . unforgettable."

"I wasn't honest about Jamie."

"That was understandable. I hold no grudge about that."

Their gazes met and held. Dario's eyes moved to her mouth and rested there. Jenna thought he was going to kiss her. She *wanted* him to kiss her. Instead, he took a deep breath and slowly exhaled. "I better get you back to the house. I'm sure everyone's worried."

The moment was gone. He lifted her in his arms and placed her on the stallion, then swung himself up behind her, wrapping one arm around her slender waist and pulling her back against his hard chest while he held the reins in the other hand.

The warmth of his bare skin seeped through the thin material of her blouse until she was more aware of Dario than of the throbbing in her ankle.

He kept the stallion at a slow gait so that her ankle wouldn't be jarred too badly. It took nearly half an hour to get back to the house, and when they finally arrived, everyone was waiting for them. Isabella and Basilio were the first out of the door. Dario tossed Basilio the reins and climbed off the horse, then pulled Jenna into his arms and carried her into the villa and up the stairs to her room. Ines followed closely behind, obviously upset.

Dario laid Jenna on the bed and then left to get some ice. Ines sat on the bed next to her, shaking her head, her dark eyes apologetic. "What can I say? I'm sorry."

"It's not your fault."

"Intellectually I know that, but emotionally I feel responsible. Did you have a run-in with Morte Negro?"

Jenna shivered involuntarily, remembering the creature's eyes. "We met all right. If Dario hadn't come when he did, I don't know what would have happened."

"I do," Ines said ominously. "I've seen what an angry bull can do to a human being."

Jenna glanced wryly at Ines. "If that was supposed to make me feel better, it didn't work."

A tiny smile touched the other woman's mouth. "Sorry, but you wouldn't believe what's been going through my mind ever since I found out they had changed Morte Negro's pasture. You were gone such a long time."

Isabella came into the room with an ace bandage and immediately began unwinding the strips of Dario's shirt from Jenna's ankle with the efficiency of a nurse. "What happened?" she asked, without looking up.

"I tripped."

"Ummmm. It's a little swollen, but not too bad yet. The ice should help."

Dario returned, and while Isabella stacked pillows under Jenna's foot to elevate it, he wrapped a towel containing ice around her ankle. "Rest now," he told her. "You may have dinner in your room this evening. I think the less you move around for the rest of the day, the better off you'll be."

"Okay." Jenna was exhausted and not about to argue.

"I'll check on you later."

Her eyes met his. "That's not necessary."

"Perhaps not for you," he said quietly, "but it is for me."

Isabella and Ines looked at one another.

When they had all gone and the door had closed behind them, Jenna tiredly closed her eyes and tried to close her mind as well. She didn't want to think about what had almost happened today. It was too horrible.

Dario returned a few hours later with Jenna's dinner. Her room was in darkness. He turned on a small light at the end of the bedroom opposite the sleeping woman and set the tray on a table, then walked to the bed where he stood looking down at her. With a gentle hand he pushed her hair off her forehead. He decided to let her sleep rather than wake her for dinner. Pulling up a chair, he sat down, his elbows on the armrests, his fingers steepled under his chin, and studied Jenna. How many times during the past three years had he closed his eyes and seen her face?

Jenna stirred. Even in sleep her ankle throbbed painfully. Her dreams were frightening. They were filled with the terrible face of Morte Negro as his hot eyes studied her. She saw his hulking mass charging Dario, sitting straight and sure on his magnificent stallion, again and again dodging the rapierlike horns of his adversary. Suddenly Dario was thrown from the horse and was lying on the ground, helpless, as the bull charged and caught him on those terrible horns.

Jenna shot up in bed, her face soaked with perspiration. She tried to scream, but no sound came out. Her eyes were wide open, but it wasn't the room she was seeing. It was Dario. He grabbed her by the shoulders and shook her until her terrified hazel eyes focused on him. Her hands clutched the front of his shirt. "Dario?"

"Yes."

"Are you all right?"

"As you can see, my Jenna, I am fine. You were dreaming."

Jenna closed her eyes, and with a long, shaking breath, pressed her cheek to his shoulder. "Hold me, please."

His arms closed securely around her, one hand stroking her silky hair. "Everything is fine," he whispered against her ear. "You're safe here, with me."

Silence filled the room.

"Do you want to talk about it?" Dario finally asked.

She shivered and he held her closer to him. "I just want to forget it."

After a time, Dario moved her slightly away from him and gazed down at her. He pushed the damp hair away from her face and kissed her forehead. "I'll be right back." Then he walked into the bathroom and came back with a cloth. Very gently he laid her back against the pillows and ran the cool cloth over her hot face.

Jenna put her hand over his and held it against her face. Her eyes were locked with his. "Don't leave me yet," she pleaded softly. "I know it was just a dream, but I don't want to be alone."

"I'll stay for as long as you want me."

Jenna took a deep breath and tiredly closed her eyes. "Thank you."

Almost an hour later, Dario's grandmother walked in and stood quietly by her grandson's chair. "How is she?"

"Her ankle is going to give her some trouble for a few days, but other than that, fine."

There was a long silence which his grandmother finally interrupted. "Don't fall in love with her, my grandson."

His eyes rested on the woman sleeping in the bed. "Your advice comes too late."

The old woman's shoulders slumped slightly forward. "What is this fascination you and your two brothers have . . . had . . . with American women? They have brought nothing but heartache into our lives. Joachim and Carlos are both dead now. Is that not enough?''

"You can't blame their deaths on the women they married."

"I *can*," she said sharply. "They didn't belong in our family." She looked down at Jenna. *"She* doesn't belong in our family."

"Jenna belongs with me, though she doesn't realize it yet. The day will come when she will be my wife. Nothing can change that."

"She isn't Portuguese."

"It doesn't matter. She's the woman I love. She's the only woman I've ever loved."

His grandmother closed her eyes for a moment, then turned and slowly walked from the room.

Jenna opened her eyes and tried to see into the dimly lit room. Dario rose from his chair and sat on the edge of the bed.

A relieved smile touched her mouth. "You're still here."

"I said I would be."

"Is it morning yet?"

"Not for a long time."

"Are you very tired?"

"No. How's your ankle?"

"It hurts like hell."

He went into the bathroom and emerged a moment later with some aspirin and a glass of water. "These should help a little," he said, lifting her into a sitting position.

She swallowed them and lay back down. Her hand found Dario's on the blanket next to her, and within minutes she was asleep again.

Chapter Five

A week after her accident, Jenna was sitting on the loggia with Basilio and speaking small, halting phrases in Portuguese. It was a very difficult language, but she was determined to learn it.

Basilio's eyes suddenly grew wide at something she said and he shouted with laughter.

A smile curved her mouth as she watched him. "What did I say?"

Again he hooted with laughter until his eyes watered.

Jenna's smile grew wider as she leaned over and touched his arm. "Come on, tell me."

Basilio wiped at his eyes with the backs of his hands. "There really isn't a translation for it. Suffice it to say that if you repeat that to anyone in public, you'll end up with a fist in your face."

"And you won't tell me?"

"Even I would blush."

A movement to her right caught Jenna's attention. She turned her head and saw Dario walking toward her, dressed in slim-fitting blue jeans and a blue oxford shirt with the sleeves pushed halfway up his forearms. It was the first time she'd seen him since the night of her accident. He sat down at the table with them, his tawny eyes on Jenna. "How's your ankle?"

"Much better. I don't even limp anymore."

"Then how would you like to go out for a ride with me?"

Her eyes lit up at the invitation. "I'd love to."

He looked over at Basilio. "Want to come with us?"

Basilio studied his friend in surprise. "Are you serious?"

A corner of Dario's mouth lifted. "Not really. Just incurably polite."

Basilio nodded in understanding. "Ah, well, in that case, perhaps some other time."

Jenna followed him down to the stables. Dario glanced at her as they walked. "Exactly how well do you ride?"

A smile tugged at her mouth. "Let's just say that what I lack in experience, I make up for in enthusiasm."

Dario's low laugh rang out, causing Jenna's smile to grow. She liked being able to make him laugh. Something told her he didn't do it very often. "While you're here I could see that you get proper riding lessons. Interested?"

"Very, thank you."

"What style of riding would you like to learn?"

"What style?"

"Western, English, Portuguese."

"Oh, Portuguese. What you did with Morte Negro was really beautiful to watch."

Dario lifted a dark brow in her direction. "You mean you'd like to learn how to fight bulls from horseback?"

"Yes." She paused. "But without the bulls."

"A novel approach."

"I like to be different."

"Do you still disapprove of Portuguese bullfighting?" he asked as he lifted his saddle from a peg on the wall and led his stallion out of one of the stalls.

"It isn't a matter of approval or disapproval," she said thoughtfully, leaning on the stall door and swinging it slightly back and forth. "Until I watched you with Morte Negro, it never occurred to me that a bullfight could be beautiful. At least the way you do it, it is. And before I always thought of the bull as the underdog."

"And now?"

"Now I understand how deadly a bull can be. I've gained respect for both the fighter and the bull."

"But you still don't like it," he finished for her.

"I don't like the idea that a man can get killed."

Dario tightened the straps around the stallion's belly. "Not if he knows what he's doing."

He finished with his stallion, then went to another stall door, led out and saddled a smaller mare for Jenna.

After giving her a foot up on the mare, Dario mounted his own horse. "What's her name?" Jenna asked, stroking the silky neck.

"*Arcogris*. It's Portuguese for 'butterfly.'"

Together, they left the stables and started across the fields of knee high grass at a rapid clip. Jenna had no trouble keeping up with Dario, but she found herself falling behind at times just so she could watch him. He sat very erect in the saddle, with one hand holding the reins and controlling the powerful horse and the other hand resting casually on his blue-jeaned leg. There was a raw strength about him that Jenna found riveting. The face he showed was unfailingly calm and reasonable. Even when he'd confronted her about Jamie, he hadn't been angry. But there was something beneath that cool facade. She had seen it in his eyes—and she wondered about it. About him. Dario Montoya was a fascinating mixture—a civilized man who fought bulls as calmly as he read stock market reports. Could one ever really know a man like that?

He dropped back until they were riding shoulder to shoulder. "Why the faraway look?" he asked.

A delicate color touched her cheeks as their eyes met. "I was just thinking some private thoughts."

He inclined his dark head. "Then I won't pry."

There was a comfortable silence between them as they rode, until Jenna broke it. "Where were you all last week?" She hadn't meant to ask that, but the words were out.

Dario didn't seem put off by the question. "I have an apartment in Lisbon. I go there at times to work."

A frown touched Jenna's forehead. "I thought the ranch was your work."

"The ranch is my hobby and my pleasure. Writing is my work."

"Writing?" She pulled the little mare up short. Dario stopped his horse as well and turned in his saddle to face her. "In all the time I've known you, you've never once mentioned that you were a writer."

He said nothing.

"What kind of writer?"

A corner of his carved mouth lifted. "A good one, I hope. I'm a historian. My most recent books have chronicled Portuguese life from the 1400s through the 1800s."

Jenna was having trouble taking this in. "How many books have you written?"

"Six."

"I'd like to read them sometime."

"They're very dry, but if you're really interested I'll have them sent to your room."

"Thank you."

He inclined his head again and kneed his horse into motion. Within the next half an hour they came to a large pasture containing a smaller enclosed area that held one horse and several men. The horse was on a lead, and it was being run in circles by first one man and then another. The men acknowledged Dario and Jenna, who sat on their horses outside the wall watching, but the work continued.

"What are they doing?"

"The horses must be perfectly trained before they can be used in a bullfight," he explained. "They must trust the rider more than their own instinct for survival. They learn to respond to the slightest touch of a rider's knee or hand, or to his tone of voice—or sometimes even just a shift in the rider's weight."

"How long does it take to train one?"

"Years." He glanced at her. "And it usually takes years to train a rider as well. Have you the patience?"

Jenna lifted her shoulders. "I honestly don't know."

"A good answer."

She watched the beautiful, aristocratic horse. "What breed are they?"

"Part Arab. Part Percheron."

And completely lovely, she thought as her eyes followed the animal's graceful movements. "Are you absolutely sure the horses don't get hurt?"

Dario laughed again and cupped the back of her head in his hand, pulling her forward until his mouth rested against her forehead. "Ah, Jenna, you are such a woman."

"You noticed."

He released her head, but his eyes remained locked with hers, his smile fading. "Oh, I noticed, Jenna Hart. A long time ago."

Jenna returned the look for as long as she could, then lowered her eyes. Dario had a way of making her feel vulnerable. And as uneasy as that vulnerability made her at times, she had to admit that she rather liked it.

When the men took a break from their work, Dario dismounted and joined them, speaking in Portuguese and listening to what they had to say about the different horses they could see in an adjoining pasture. Jenna remained on her horse and watched. The sun reflected off Dario's thick, dark hair. He was a head taller than most of the men but didn't stoop to speak with them. Jenna found herself smiling as she watched him and had no idea why. Perhaps it was just because he made her feel good.

Dario returned a few minutes later and mounted his horse, then looked over at her. "Hungry?"

"Ravenous."

"I know a shortcut to a small restaurant. What would you say to getting a picnic lunch there and then taking it to the cool banks of a stream to eat?"

"I'd like that."

He wheeled the big stallion around. "Let's go, then."

The two of them raced like the wind across the fields. Jenna felt more alive than she had in years with the wind

whipping her golden hair straight back and the hot
Portuguese sun beating down on her. She had a little
trouble keeping up with Dario, and even at that she sensed
that he was holding the stallion back from his full stride. It
seemed like no time at all before they left the fields to ride
along a deserted gravel road. After only a few minutes on
the road, they came upon a wooden shack. The delicious
smell of food scented the air around it. Jenna's stomach
rumbled impatiently.

Dario helped her down from her horse, his hands warm
at her waist. He didn't drop them right away, but stood
looking down at her. Jenna became more and more aware
of his touch. Her breathing grew shallow as his gaze
lingered on her mouth. His hands pulled her closer then
slid around to her back and held her against him.

An enormously overweight Portuguese woman rushed
out of the shack toward them and the moment was over.
As Dario turned from her to be grabbed by the woman in a
bear hug, Jenna closed her eyes and pressed her hand
against her pounding heart. Aerobics had nothing on
Dario Montoya when it came to exercising the heart.

Dario and the woman spoke in the rapid Portuguese she
was becoming accustomed to hearing, and then Dario
introduced them, explaining to Jenna that his friend spoke
no English at all.

In the shack the woman chattered happily the entire
time she packed their basket with food and wine, but even
so, they were on their way again in half an hour. They
rode back onto Dario's land and to a cool, clear stream
with grassy banks and trees for shade. When they had
dismounted, Dario unsaddled the horses and tethered them
loosely so they could graze easily and reach the water.

While he was busy with the horses, Jenna spread out a cloth the woman had packed and began setting out their lunch—right down to the wine in paper cups. Dario sat next to her, his eyes on her bent head as she worked. Jenna was aware of his look, but there was no break in her motions. When she had finished, she handed him one of the paper cups and lifted hers to his in a brief toast. "To a pleasant afternoon. Thank you."

Dario inclined his head, his eyes steadily on hers as they drank. Then he set his cup down and lay back on the cloth, one hand behind his head as, with a sigh, he closed his eyes.

Jenna quietly nibbled bread and cheese as she watched him. He looked tired. She found herself worrying about whether or not he got enough rest. Before long she realized that he was asleep. His carved face relaxed, but there was still a small frown on the bridge of his nose, as though something bothered him, even in his sleep.

She rose quietly after a time and wandered down to the stream where she rolled up the legs of her jeans and went wading in the cool water, occasionally scooping some up in her hands and splashing it on her warm skin.

The afternoon passed quietly. Even the birds seemed to be napping in order to avoid the heat. Shafts of light, narrow at the top and wide at the bottom, broke through the trees to sweep the ground. Jenna, loathe to wake Dario, wandered around for a long time before coming back and sitting beside him. Her gaze roamed leisurely over his face, enjoying the freedom to look at will.

Dario moved slightly and turned his head. Slowly his eyes opened right into hers. "Hello," he said in a low voice after a moment.

"Hello," Jenna answered softly.

"Did I sleep long?"

"A couple of hours."

"You should have awakened me."

She shook her head. "You needed the rest."

"So now you worry not only about the bull and the horse, but the bullfighter as well."

She smiled. "I'm a born mother."

His eyes were still on her. "I don't need a mother, Jenna."

Jenna's eyes dropped. She didn't know how to answer.

Dario put a gentle finger under her chin and forced her to look at him. "Why do you keep shying away from me? When I touch you, I can feel you respond."

"I'm attracted to you," she admitted. And then with a charming smile. "I'm *very* attracted to you."

"But?"

She lifted her shoulders, as though looking for the answer herself. "I don't know you. I don't know anything of what you think or feel."

"I am a very boring man."

"Oh, I don't think so," she said dryly.

His finger moved lightly over her jaw. "Jenna, I am what you see. I have some secrets in my life, but then everyone does."

Jenna studied him with thoughtful hazel eyes. "Do you mind if I ask you a very personal question?"

He waited.

"Were you in love with Elisa when she died."

"No."

She remembered the look on his face when he had spoken of her death. Something had been there.

Dario read her thoughts. "What I felt," he explained,

"was guilt. Elisa still pined for Carlos when we were first married, but she got over him."

"You mean that she fell in love with you?"

"And I couldn't return even a little of her feeling. All I could offer her was my friendship and some affection."

A frown creased Jenna's forehead, and Dario smoothed it away with his thumb.

"It wasn't a marriage in name only," he explained. "I was her husband in every sense of the word. But I couldn't love her because I was in love with someone else when I married her."

"Did she know that?"

"I told her."

"And she married you anyway?"

"She knew I would make an honest effort in the marriage. At first it didn't matter to her that there was no love."

"And yet you slept with her." Jenna was hurt by this, as though he had betrayed her—and the fact that none of this had anything to do with her in the least didn't seem to matter.

"Jenna, when I married her, as far as I knew, it was going to be for the rest of my life. It wasn't something I entered into lightly, and I treated it as a real marriage. I don't think I need to apologize for that."

Her eyes dropped again. "No, of course you don't. It isn't any of my business anyway. I shouldn't have asked."

"Of course you should have," he disagreed. "I want us always to be able to talk about anything."

Jenna's teeth tugged on her lower lip. "Whatever happened to the woman you were in love with?" she asked.

Dario's hand slid around to the back of her head and

pulled her face close to his. "Some day I'll tell you all about her."

His mouth lingeringly caressed hers. With a deft motion, he rolled her onto her back and looked deeply into her eyes. It was then that Jenna knew. *She* was the woman. He looked at her with a hunger and tenderness that had started a long time ago, not just since she'd arrived in Portugal. And she responded to it.

A gentle warmth rose in her and spread as their tongues mingled and the kiss deepened passionately. Dario kissed a moist path down her pulsing throat to the soft skin between her breasts. His hand worked her blouse out of her jeans and unbuttoned it with the careless assurance of experience. His warm fingers trailed over her smooth skin with a gentle reverence that made her overwhelmingly aware of her body and his touch. His mouth brushed the swell of her breast, circling, until he found her nipple, hardened with the desire he had stirred.

Jenna arched beneath him, reveling in the physical need this man aroused in her. Her fingers tangled in his thick hair and pulled his mouth back to hers. His shirt was unbuttoned and as his mouth recaptured hers, his smoothly muscled torso pressed and rubbed against hers.

He kissed the corners of her mouth and then buried his face in her neck and lay still. He could feel her tremble beneath him, and it told him more of her innocence than words ever could have. It also brought him back to his senses.

Tenderly he gathered Jenna into his arms and rolled onto his side, taking her with him so that they lay facing each other.

Jenna's hazel eyes searched his. "Why did you stop?"

He pushed the hair away from her face. "Because in a

few minutes I wouldn't have been able to, and I don't think you're ready for that yet."

A smile touched her mouth. "Ever the honorable man."

But he wasn't teasing her. "Jenna, when we make love—and we will—it has to be right for both of us, or it won't be right for either." He pulled her back into his arms until their bodies once again pressed against each other, then got abruptly to his feet, pulling Jenna up after him. As Jenna watched him, he put his hands between her breasts and, button by button, fastened her blouse. Then he unsnapped her jeans and pulled her against him as he tucked her blouse in the back and then the front. She felt the pressure against her stomach as he refastened her jeans, and then slowly zipped them. His hand tenderly touched her cheek. "What's going on behind those beautiful eyes of yours?"

"A hundred different things."

Dario trailed the back of his hand down her cheek.

Jenna cupped her hand over his and turned her face to kiss his palm. "I'm very vulnerable around you. Thank you for understanding that and not moving too fast for me." She sighed and again searched his face. "Am I in love with you, Dario Montoya?"

The grooves in his cheeks deepened. "Am I supposed to tell you?"

"I wish you could."

"I wish I could, too," he said quietly, and then walked across to his horse. "We'd better get back to the house. Everyone will be worried."

It was late in the afternoon when they walked into the villa. Tomaso walked up to Jenna and gave her a crisp bow. "While you were out a woman named Christy called and wants you to call her back immediately."

She glanced up at Dario. "I hope they haven't run into a problem with the fashion show."

"There's only one way to find out. Use the phone in my library. You'll have some privacy there."

"Thank you." She started to walk away from him, but turned suddenly, her lovely face serious. They looked at each other for a timeless interval. Then she left.

Still thoughtful, Jenna found her way to the library and sat down at Dario's heavy mahogany desk. A few moments later she had Christy on the line. She relaxed back in the leather chair. "I just got your message. Is something wrong?"

"Jenna! I didn't think you'd ever call me back!" came Christy's frantic voice. "We have a problem. You have to come home."

Jenna sat up. "What kind of problem?"

"Three of our biggest buyers from last year said that either you be here so that they can deal with both of us directly, or they'll take their business elsewhere."

"That's absurd."

"Of course it is, but I'm not about to tell *them* that. What the customer wants, the customer gets, and in this instance they want *both* of us. You'll be here, won't you?"

Jenna sighed. She felt as though she'd just arrived in Portugal. "Of course I'll be there. The show is in a little over two weeks. When do you want me in Chicago?"

"Tomorrow." Christy's answer was completely without hesitation.

"Tomorrow!"

"Listen, Jenna, things are crazy. I can't do this without you. I thought I could, but I can't. If you don't get here and get here soon I'm going to go over the edge. Ken is driving me up the wall. He may be a whiz as a business manager, but he doesn't know the first thing about fashion shows. Which would be okay if he *realized* it, but he doesn't. He's going to ruin everything without you to hold him in check."

Jenna laughed at her friend. "All right, all right. I'll be there sometime tomorrow."

Christy let out a long breath. "Thank heavens. So," she continued as though her near hysteria of a few moments before hadn't happened, "how is Jamie doing?"

A soft smile touched Jenna's mouth. "He's thriving. Never was a child surrounded by more love and attention."

"So you did the right thing."

"I did the right thing—perhaps for both Jamie and me."

"Come again?"

"I'll explain when I see you."

"Tomorrow, right?" She still needed reassurance.

"Tomorrow."

"And tonight I'll be able to sleep for the first time since you left this madhouse."

"Sweet dreams."

"Goodnight, Jenna."

Jenna thoughtfully hung up the phone and started to rise from the chair, but a file on Dario's desk caught her eye. It was labeled "Jamie—Adoption." With only the slightest hesitation at poking her nose into someone else's private files, she opened it and stared with disbelieving eyes at papers which gave Dario legal adoptive custody of Jamie. He had legally taken Jamie away from her and hadn't said a word!

And he had known that even as they were together by the stream. She was shocked at the betrayal. Why would he do something like that? She studied the papers again. There had to be some explanation, some reasonable explanation.

Even as these thoughts whirled in her head, the study door opened and Dario stepped in. His eyes went from her hurt ones to the file she held in her hand. He let out a long breath and closed the door behind him. "Don't look at me like that, Jenna. It's not what you think."

She tossed the file onto the desk as Dario walked across the room toward her. "Why didn't you tell me you were adopting Jamie?"

"Because I was hoping adoption wouldn't be necessary. I'm still hoping. If you examined the file, you will have noticed that the papers aren't signed—and they are in English. I wanted you to understand them."

"I thought we agreed to informal joint custody. This would give you complete control over Jamie."

"Legally. But our private agreement would still stand."

"Then why bother with the adoption?"

He waved her back into the chair and then sat on the edge of the desk facing her. "Do you remember in Chicago when I asked you if you had found a copy of Carlos and Caroline's marriage certificate among your sister's things?"

Jenna nodded. "And I said that I hadn't."

"That's right. And I didn't find one in Carlos' things either. You also said that you weren't a witness to the

1. How do you rate _____
   (Please print book TITLE)

   1.6 ☐ excellent   .4 ☐ good   .2 ☐ not so good

   .5 ☐ very good   .3 ☐ fair   .1 ☐ poor

2. How likely are you to purchase another book:
   in this *series* ?   by this *author* ?

   2.1 ☐ definitely would purchase   3.1 ☐ definitely would purchase

   .2 ☐ probably would puchase   .2 ☐ probably would puchase

   .3 ☐ probably would not purchase   .3 ☐ probably would not purchase

   .4 ☐ definitely would not purchase   .4 ☐ definitely would not purchase

   Q12

3. How does this book compare with similar books you usually read?

   4.1 ☐ far better than others   .2 ☐ better than others   .3 ☐ about the

   .4 ☐ not as good   .5 ☐ definitely not as good   same

4. Please check the statements you feel best describe this book.

   5. ☐ Easy to read   6. ☐ Too much violence/anger

   7. ☐ Realistic conflict   8. ☐ Wholesome/not too sexy

   9. ☐ Too sexy   10. ☐ Interesting characters

   11. ☐ Original plot   12. ☐ Especially romantic

   13. ☐ Not enough humor   14. ☐ Difficult to read

   15. ☐ Didn't like the subject   16. ☐ Good humor in story

   17. ☐ Too predictable   18. ☐ Not enough description of setting

   19. ☐ Believable characters   20. ☐ Fast paced

   21. ☐ Couldn't put the book down   22. ☐ Heroine too juvenile/weak/silly

   23. ☐ Made me feel good   24. ☐ Too many foreign/unfamiliar words

   25. ☐ Hero too dominating   26. ☐ Too wholesome/not sexy enough

   27. ☐ Not enough romance   28. ☐ Liked the setting

   29. ☐ Ideal hero   30. ☐ Heroine too independent

   31. ☐ Slow moving   32. ☐ Unrealistic conflict

   33. ☐ Not enough suspense   34. ☐ Sensuous/not too sexy

   35. ☐ Liked the subject   36. ☐ Too much description of setting

5. What *most* prompted you to buy this book?

   37. ☐ Read others in series   38. ☐ Title   39. ☐ Cover art

   40. ☐ Friend's recommendation   41. ☐ Author   42. ☐ In-store display

   43. ☐ TV, radio or magazine ad   44. ☐ Price   45. ☐ Story outline

   46. ☐ Ad inside other books   47. ☐ Other _____ (please specify)

6. Please indicate how many romance paperbacks you read in a month.

   48.1 ☐ 1 to 4   .2 ☐ 5 to 10   .3 ☐ 11 to 15   .4 ☐ more than 15

7. Please indicate your sex and age group.

   49.1 ☐ Male   50.1 ☐ under 15   .3 ☐ 25-34   .5 ☐ 50-64

   .2 ☐ Female   .2 ☐ 15-24   .4 ☐ 35-49   .6 ☐ 65 or older

8. Have you any additional comments about this book?

   _____ (51)

   _____ (53)

Thank you for completing and returning this questionnaire.

Printed in USA

NAME _____
          (Please Print)
ADDRESS _____
CITY _____
ZIP CODE _____

POSTAGE WILL BE PAID BY ADDRESSEE

BUSINESS REPLY MAIL
FIRST CLASS   PERMIT NO. 70   TEMPE, AZ.

NATIONAL READER SURVEYS
2504 West Southern Avenue
Tempe, AZ   85282

marriage and that, in fact, they had disappeared for a few days and, upon their return, announced that they were married.''

''So?''

''So, if Jamie is to inherit his father's holdings in this ranch, his legitimacy has to be proved or they revert to me. The adoption protects Jamie. If he is my son, he will be an unchallenged Montoya. When I die, he will inherit not only his father's holdings, but mine as well. Without the adoption, unless and until the marriage certificate is found, he has a right to nothing, not even his name.''

''But they were married, I'm sure of it. Caroline was ecstatic.''

''And eventually the detectives I've hired will find out where and when, but until then other steps may have to be taken. I wasn't trying to deceive you. I would have told you before signing.''

Jenna met his direct gaze with one of her own. ''I know that. I was just a little surprised when I saw the papers. You've been more than fair in allowing me to live here with Jamie, when you could have cut me out of his life altogether.'' Her eyes dropped.

''Did you call Christy?'' he asked, changing the subject.

''Right before you came in. I have to leave for Chicago tomorrow. She's having trouble with some buyers—and with Ken.''

''How long will you be gone?''

''Probably three weeks.''

''That's a long time. Jamie will miss you.''

''I'll miss him, too.'' And you, Dario Montoya, she thought to herself. And you.

''I'll call my pilot.''

Jenna hadn't thought about that. She touched his arm and shook her head. "No, please don't do that. Your offer is generous, but I'd prefer using a commercial airline."

A corner of his mouth lifted. "There are no strings attached to my offer."

"I know, but I'd prefer to pay my own way. And when I return, I'd like to talk to you about sharing Jamie's expenses."

"This is important to you?"

"Very."

He inclined his dark head in a gesture she was becoming familiar with. "Then so be it. We shall share equally in all things concerning our nephew."

Jenna smiled at him with a smile that reached her lovely eyes. The man found himself lost for a moment.

She rose from the chair and started to leave the room, but turned at the door. "Will I see you at dinner?"

Dario looked at her. "I'm having dinner with Basilio tonight."

Jenna's heart fell a little. "Oh. Well, I guess I'll see you when I get back in three weeks." She turned to leave again, but Dario's voice stopped her.

"Jenna, I could cancel my dinner, but I think it's best for both of us if I don't."

She studied him quietly. "Why?"

He moved closer until he stood directly in front of her. "Because," he said with soft intensity, "I can't be with you without wanting to make love to you. Because I know that tonight everyone but the two of us will be out of the house and that we will end up in each other's arms." His gaze cherished her. "Because I ache with the need I feel for you, but I know you aren't ready yet." He reached out with a gentle hand and cupped her cheek. "And that is why I will be having dinner with Basilio tonight."

Jenna tossed and turned that night. Hours passed before she finally gave in to her sleeplessness, got up and dressed in a loose skirt and blouse, then headed outside into the garden. The moon was full and bright, lighting smooth grass paths through thickly growing flowers and sculpted bushes. Jenna stopped with her hands on her slender hips and took a deep breath of the fragrant air. There was such peace here at night. It was almost intoxicating.

"Hello, dear." A voice sliced into the silence.

Jenna jumped and turned, her hand over her heart. "Oh, Senhora Montoya! I didn't see you sitting there."

"And I've frightened you. I'm so sorry." She patted the bench next to her. "Come, keep an old woman company."

Jenna sat down. "Do you come out here like this often?"

She could feel the Senhora's smile through the dark. "Almost every night. One of the curses of old age is, unfortunately, insomnia."

"Believe me," Jenna sympathized, "it isn't just a curse of old age."

A comfortable silence fell between them as they both enjoyed their surroundings. "I understand," the Senhora finally said, "that you are returning to your home tomorrow. I hope it's nothing serious . . . ?"

"No. Just business."

"So you will be . . . coming back here?"

Jenna turned and looked at the Senhora's profile. "Of course. Jamie is here. Wherever he is, is where I belong."

She met Jenna's gaze. "May I speak frankly?"

"I wish you would."

"Thank you." She took a deep breath and looked back into the moonlit garden. "I think it would be best for all concerned if you kept America as your permanent home and confined yourself to short visits here to see Jamie."

Jenna was really surprised by the woman's words. She'd honestly thought Senhora Montoya liked her. "Why?"

"Because of Dario. I don't want to see him involved with you. Not because of you personally, please understand. I'm sure you're a fine person. I just don't want to see him fall in love with an American. I've seen two of my grandson's lives destroyed by American women. I would like Dario spared."

"What do you mean destroyed by American women? You make us sound like some kind of plague."

"And so you have been to my family. First Dario's older brother, Joachim. He traveled to America and fell in love with a woman there. She was a professional woman, like yourself. Joachim was old-fashioned. He never adjusted to having his wife working like a man, traveling here and there whenever she chose without a thought to my grandson and his needs. She had no interest in having children. What she *was* interested in, though, was other men. He died on the horns of a bull because his thoughts were on his wife instead of on what he was doing."

"I didn't know Dario had had an older brother. I'm sorry for what happened, but you can hardly paint all American women with the same brush—"

"Then," the woman continued without listening to Jenna, "there was Carlos and your sister. Because of her, he not only broke his solemn word to his betrothed, but he was alienated from his family and his country. He, too, is now dead.''

"He was in love with Caroline. She made him happy."

"So you told me when you arrived." Suddenly she turned to Jenna and took one of the young woman's hands between her two wrinkled ones. Her brown eyes were pleading. "I have seen how you look at Dario. I have seen how he looks at you. But I also see that the two of you couldn't be more wrong for each other. He needs a woman who understands our ways. He needs a woman like Ines."

"He doesn't love her."

"But he could learn to if you were to leave here for good." She rose from the bench, patting Jenna's hand and placing it back in the young woman's lap. "Think on my words, dear. My grandson is not for you."

Jenna sat there in complete astonishment after the Senhora had gone. What had just happened here? One minute she was made to feel like part of the family and the next she was asked to leave. She got up and stuffed her hands deep into the pockets of her skirt as she once again wandered the garden paths. She couldn't walk away from Dario. There was something between them which neither of them could ignore. She had to find out if it was more powerful than their differences.

Chapter Six

Three weeks later Jenna's plane circled high above the twinkling lights of Lisbon before finally landing. She sat still long after the plane stopped and waited patiently while the other passengers got off, almost too tired to get her things together. Her trip to Chicago had been hectic and exhausting. The show had gone beautifully, but not without a few glitches, and not without enormous effort on everyone's part. And after the show came the rush to make sure everyone's orders could be filled with the high quality of clothing that was now expected of Hart-Windom. She couldn't remember the last time she'd had a really good night's sleep.

And all the time Senhora Montoya's words echoed in her mind. Should she stay away?

Wearily she unfastened her seatbelt and picked up her briefcase and shoulder bag. She was the last one off the plane. When she walked into the terminal, the first person she saw was Dario, leaning against a pillar, his arms folded across his chest, his eyes on her. Jenna's steps faltered. She hadn't expected to be met by anyone, much less Dario. No one knew she was returning tonight. A sudden energy filled her. She didn't wonder at it. All she knew was that there wasn't anyone she wanted to see more.

As she approached, Dario moved away from the pillar, his eyes never leaving her face. "Hello, Jenna."

Her mouth curved into a lovely smile. "Hello, Dario. How did you know to meet me tonight?"

"I called Chicago and spoke with Christy. She told me which plane you'd be on." He reached out a gentle hand and touched the shadows under her eyes. "You look tired."

"I was until a few minutes ago. I seem to have gotten my second wind."

"Do you think this second wind will last long enough for us to have dinner together in Lisbon?"

"I guarantee it."

He took her briefcase and put his hand under her arm. Quickly they walked through Customs. The official didn't even look at her before stamping her passport. Within minutes they were alone in Dario's car and heading for the Alfama, or old Lisbon. They parked in a cobblestone area at the bottom of a hill and stepped out into a surprisingly cool night. Again Dario took her arm and they walked up through a narrow cobblestone maze, flanked on both sides by simple two-story buildings, most of which had colorful flower boxes below the windows. In some places the road narrowed so much that it seemed possible for people living across the street from one another to reach out their windows and shake hands.

The Alfama was a crowded place, even at that late hour. Music came pouring out of the *fado* bars, their doors open to the fresh night air. Couples stood in doorways, talking in hushed voices. Groups of handsome men, four abreast, laughing quietly, passed them, some turning to admire Jenna, others too shy to show so obvious an interest.

When they came to a very small, clean-looking building with a simple painted sign which said "Malmequer/ Bemequer," Dario stopped. He opened the door for her, and Jenna entered one of the smallest, most charming restaurants she'd ever been in. There were only five tables, each covered with a black-and-white checkered tablecloth that was topped by a snowy white cloth. A young man, dressed in neat, faded jeans, a white shirt and black tie, who obviously knew Dario, stepped forward and greeted him, then turned to Jenna for an introduction. He went from Portuguese to English without hesitation and seated them with an elegant flourish. Within moments he returned with a bottle of wine which he poured for both of them. Then he left to wait on the other two couples who were in the restaurant.

Dario lifted his glass to Jenna. "To the loveliest woman in Portugal."

Her cheeks pinkened slightly as she acknowledged the compliment and sipped her wine.

"What are you thinking about?" Dario asked suddenly, leaning comfortably back in his chair.

Jenna relaxed also and gazed around the restaurant. "I was thinking how different the Portuguese people are from what I expected."

"And what did you expect?"

"Oh," she said thoughtfully, "I don't really know. I suppose I was expecting a little more Latin exuberance."

"We are not really Latin here."

"Explain it to me, then. What exactly is a Portuguese?"

He smiled. "An interesting question." He paused for a moment and studied the ruby color of the wine in his glass. "We are predominantly an Atlantic and *not* a Mediterranean people. Our temperament has very little in common with that of Italians. For the most part we are introverted and reserved. We have a horror of making spectacles of ourselves, unlike most Latins. If there is one quality which is undeniably Portuguese, it is *saudades*. *Saudades* is a state of longing—for a person or a place. It's a bittersweet feeling which fills all of the Portuguese at one time or another—an inexplicable sadness which goes as quickly as it comes."

Jenna tilted her golden head to one side. "You mean depression?"

"No, no. Not at all." He leaned forward, as though to make her better understand what he was saying. "It is part of the Portuguese character. We have in us a sense of loss. Of things past that will never return. It is a recurrent theme in our history and our literature." His eyes met hers. "Do you understand?"

Jenna leaned forward as well. "Yes, I do. It makes the Portuguese seem mysterious." She found the conversation really interesting. "How else would you describe your people?"

"All that and she wants more!" He smiled at her and sipped his wine. "Well, we are fiercely loyal, and therefore exceptionally hurt by a betrayal of any kind. We are a sentimental and kind people with the very human love of a good scandal. We are brave and tenacious, as our history shows. We are honorable."

She thought of his marriage to Elisa. "Yes," she said thoughtfully, "you are certainly that."

The waiter came to their table with two plates heaped with a delicious smelling lamb curry over a fluffy bed of rice. Jenna thought she was in heaven.

The grooves in Dario's cheeks deepened as he watched her. "One would think you hadn't eaten since you left here three weeks ago."

She took another bite and savored it for a moment. "Ummm. I haven't really. Just snacks and quick sandwiches. There was no time."

"I take it the show went well."

"Very. Our profits for this season should be better than last season by nearly twenty percent."

"That's an impressive growth."

"And we earned every penny of it."

"And now I suppose you have to begin work on next season's line of clothes."

She sipped her ice water. "It's neverending."

"And you love every moment of it."

Her smile enchanted him. "I do." But even through the conversation, his grandmother's words rang in her ears.

Suddenly Dario reached out and took her hand. "On the outside you smile, but inside," his hand touched the spot between her breasts where her heart beat so steadily, "you are pensive. What is it?"

"Perhaps it's a little of that Portuguese *saudades* you were describing to me before."

"I think it's more. Tell me."

Jenna's eyes met his. She didn't want secrets between them ever again. "I had a talk with your grandmother the night before I went to Chicago."

"And?"

the door, then turned to her. "You undoubtedly want to see Jamie."

She smiled at him. "I promise not to wake him. I'd just like to see for myself that he's all right."

Dario put his arm around her waist as they walked to the baby's room and tiptoed to the crib. The nurse slept soundly on the other side of the room. A small nightlight on a table next to the crib gave off just enough light so that they could make out Jamie's dark little head on the white pillow. The urge to pick him up and hug him was almost overwhelming for Jenna, but that would only wake him. Instead, she leaned over and rested her cheek on his soft warm one and sighed. Three weeks was too long a time to have been away. Christy and Ken were going to have to learn to be a little more independent.

With another sigh, she straightened away from the baby and gently lifted the blanket to his small shoulders. Dario stood behind her, his hands on her arms, and pulled her back against him. "It's good to be home, isn't it?" he whispered above her ear.

She tilted the back of her head against his chest and looked up at him. "Did you doubt it?"

His smile touched her as he guided her to the door and closed it gently behind them. When Jenna continued on to her room, Dario reached out and caught her hand, turning her around and into his arms. For a long time he just looked into her eyes, trying to read her soul. "What am I going to do with you, woman?" he finally asked, his voice a little gruff.

The dimple in her left cheek appeared. "What would you like to do with me?"

"I'd like to kiss you, like this." His mouth captured hers, gently at first, tenderly. Then the kiss deepened until

Jenna was on her toes, her arms around his neck, trying to get deeper inside him, unable to get close enough. "And then," he said as he raised his mouth from hers and trailed it along her jaw to her ear where she could feel his warm breath, "I'd like to kiss you here." Jenna closed her eyes. Her ears were remarkably sensitive—and to think she hadn't known that until now.

His hand lifted her heavy hair and his mouth left her ear to explore the back of her neck. Jenna's fingers dug into his shoulders as a soft moan escaped her parted lips. Was there no part of her body immune to him?

"Dario," she finally managed to whisper. "Dario?"

He left the back of her neck to look down into her heavy-lidded eyes. "Do you want me to stop?"

She nodded. Then shook her head. "Oh," she finally told him in her forthright fashion, "what I really want is to be carried off by you and kissed until I'm beyond thought. But I think you were right about waiting."

Dario pulled her into his arms and held her quietly. "It's hard, though, knowing that you're sleeping alone, so near where I am sleeping alone."

He walked her to her room and opened the door for her. "I'll see you in the morning." Without another word, he closed the door between them. She heard him walk down the stairs rather than to his room. Somewhere in the house a door closed. Leaving her room in darkness, she walked to her window and opened it. The cool night air lifted the curtains as she sat on the window seat hugging her knees to her chest, staring out over the moonlit grounds. The minutes ticked by as she sat there. Suddenly she noticed a movement by the stables and recognized Dario in the moonlight. He disappeared inside, then came out seconds later leading his saddleless stallion. In one graceful movement he leaped on the horse's back, and horse and rider vanished into the distance.

Jenna stared after them long after they had gone. Then, with a tired sigh, she leaned her head back and closed her eyes. She had done it. She had fallen in love with Dario Montoya all over again. Only this time it went way beyond infatuation.

Her eyes narrowed into the distance, searching for one last glimpse of Dario, but he had vanished. With a sigh that started at her toes, she walked to the bed and all but fell onto it, still in her clothes. Within seconds she was sound asleep.

Dario rode fast and hard, stopping only when he sensed that his stallion needed a rest. The two of them sat stone still in the middle of the pasture, silhouetted by the full moon. A muscle worked in Dario's jaw. Jenna was coming around. But he had a gut feeling that something was going to keep them apart again, and it ate at him.

When she heard Dario's knock the next morning, Jenna rolled over, hugging her pillow. "Go away!"

He opened the door and walked over to her bed. Jamie was grinning from the backcarrier strapped on Dario's shoulders. "Now how can you possibly tell the two men in your life to go away."

Jenna looked at them dolefully with one eye as she pointed to her lips. "Go a-way," she enunciated very clearly.

Dario reached over his head and lifted Jamie out of the carrier, then set him on top of Jenna. "Time for the big guns, I see.'' Jamie wrapped his little arms around her neck and Jenna glared at Dario over the baby's dark head.

"Unfair tactics,'' she charged, a smile in her voice as her arms wrapped around his little body.

Dario laughed. "Whatever works.''

"What time is it?''

"Ten o'clock. The parade starts in less than two hours.''

She held Jamie out to him. "If you two gentlemen will excuse me, I'll be ready in a few minutes.''

Quickly she put on a gathered grape-colored cotton skirt and a short-sleeved white blouse. After running a quick brush through her blond hair, she held it away from her face with a narrow plastic band. As she was putting on a pale rose lipstick, her hand stopped in midair as she looked at herself in the mirror. Her cheeks were flushed; her hazel eyes were bright. A smile seemed to be tugging at the corners of her mouth. Jenna finished putting on the lipstick and hummed as she capped it and put it back on the dresser. This was Dario's doing. She had never looked lovelier. She had never been happier.

She never wanted it to end.

The sound of a car horn brought her back to her surroundings. With a smile at Dario's impatience, she grabbed her shoulder bag and left her room with a light step.

Dario was standing beside the open passenger door, leaning on it as he waited for her. Jamie was already strapped into the carseat. Jenna stood in front of Dario, on the other side of the door and impulsively stood on her toes and kissed him tenderly on the mouth. "I think I'm falling in love with you,'' she whispered.

With their faces still close, Dario trailed a finger down

her cheek. "When you're sure, let me know and we'll talk."

"I'll do that."

He closed the door after her and climbed behind the wheel. Within minutes they were off the ranch and on the road to Santarem. The land was flat and the scenery lush in this part of Portugal, though in other parts, you could see scenery of almost any description. Portugal, Jenna was discovering, was a country of rich and varied beauty.

When they got to Santarem, she was surprised at how busy it was. Crowds of cars and people, all in town for the parade, cluttered the streets. Dario miraculously found a parking space. A few moments later Jamie was happily riding in the carrier on Dario's shoulders, and the three of them were slowly making their way through the city. "We have time for some sightseeing. Interested?"

She was busy examining the front of an ancient hotel and nodded absently. With a smile, Dario took her arm and led her through the people. A street vendor was selling flowers. Dario stopped and bought a red rose which he tucked in Jenna's hair with infinite tenderness. His tawny eyes rested on her mouth. "You should always wear flowers in your hair."

Her heart started that rapid beating again. Did he know what it did to her when he looked at her like that? she wondered.

Dario led her to a small church. They stood in front of it for a moment. "This is called S. Joao de Alporao. It was turned into a museum of sorts some years ago." Inside they found the tomb of a knight, his naked sword raised in one hand as if about to strike down some infidel or other. "Who is he?" Jenna whispered, feeling the hush surrounding them.

"Dom Duarte de Menese, Count of Viana. He was killed by the Moors. Only a tooth remained when they had finished with him."

A shiver of horror ran through Jenna.

Dario sensed her distaste. "Violent death was common in those days." He shrugged. "Even today it is sometimes a sad fact of life."

Jenna's thoughts immediately turned to bullfighting, and again Dario read her mind as though it were his own. She felt his eyes on her. "You worry too much, Jenna Hart."

There wasn't much else to see in the little museum, except for a few *azulejos* on the walls, coins and prehistoric implements. The place had the air of a studio in which a mess of litter surrounds a once lovely object. And yet she liked it. It was comfortable rather than impressive, like so many of the museums in Portugal.

With fingers twined, they walked back into the bright and dusty Portuguese day. Jamie's wide eyes took in everything and everyone as they moved through the city. Finally they stopped before a church called the Ingreja da Graca. The doorway had an arched and pointed entrance, like the entrance to a cave. In the plain wall above the portal was a rose window which caught and held Jenna's attention. "It looks as though it's revolving," she finally decided.

Dario studied it as well. "I never noticed that until now, but yes, it does."

Walking down the long flight of steps inside the clean, scrubbed and empty church, she felt like a swimmer, walking into deep, cold water. It was so very, very still. And there was no place to hide from the white stare of the altar.

Here they found yet another tomb, this one of Dom Pedro de Meneses, Count of Viana, and his Lady. For some reason, Jenna found herself smiling at the couple.

"I feel that about them, also," Dario told her. "They are almost like friends."

Jenna felt a sudden chill. "I'd like to go back outside."

When they got back into the sun, Jenna breathed deeply of the warm air. Somewhere in the distance came the sounds of bands warming up. Dario looked down at her and smiled. "Are you ready?"

Jenna's eyes narrowed suspiciously. "Is there something about this parade you haven't told me?"

Dario looked blandly down at her. "Let's just say that you haven't seen a parade until you've seen a Portuguese one. And heard one," he added for good measure.

Jenna put her hand on Dario's shoulder and Jamie grabbed one of her fingers to hold on to. A moment later a group of lovely young girls dressed in brightly colored robes with flowers in their dark hair walked by scattering flowers and carrying palm leaves. Behind them came a group of men carrying an elaborate litter with the image of the Virgin on it, closely followed by more litters with more saints. Then came the clergymen carrying silver crowns on black cushions.

Jenna was completely charmed, and when three hopelessly out of tune brass bands marched by, all playing their hearts out—and playing different songs—her heart was completely won over.

Following the bands were several bullock with gilded horns and garlanded heads. Jenna cheered and applauded with the rest of the noisy crowd as Dario watched her.

When the last of the parade had gone by, he took her hand and they started back to the car. The manners of the

Portuguese people were amazing. Even here, where there was much bumping and pushing, it was done with humor and apologies.

Dario got Jamie strapped into the carseat, then climbed in next to Jenna. She smiled over at him. "What shall we do now?"

"Unfortunately I have to take you home."

"What about you?"

"I have some work to do on the ranch. With the bullfights in three days, I have to make sure the ring is ready and get the right bulls lined up."

Jenna just stared at him, her smile fading. "What bullfights?"

"For the fiesta."

"I hate to sound redundant, but what fiesta?"

"I'm sorry, Jenna. I just assumed you knew. At this time every year the Montoyas have a fiesta. There is dancing, singing, eating, drinking . . ."

"And bullfighting," she finished for him.

"And bullfighting. The buyers of our stock come from Mexico, Spain and all across Portugal to watch the bulls and the horses, and to select the stock they want."

"I was under the impression that once a bull had been in the ring it was dangerous to use him again."

"They don't buy the bulls they see in the ring. That is purely a spectacle. The best matadors in the world will be there, doing what they do so well. The bulls will be representative of their sires and the buyers will be able to judge other bulls based on the performance of the bulls used in the ring."

"It's a complicated process."

"Not if you know what you're doing."

Silence filled the car as he maneuvered patiently

through the heavy traffic. Suddenly Jenna turned to him. "I'd like to go to the bullring with you."

Dario glanced at her out of the corner of his eye. "Why?"

"I'd just like to see it."

"You're lying."

Jenna turned in her seat so she could look at him. "You're going to be in that bullfight, aren't you?"

"A Montoya always is. It's part of the tradition."

She touched his arm. "I've never seen a bullring. I've never seen a bullfight. I'd like to know a little about what I can expect because I don't want to sit around worried sick for three days beforehand, all right?"

Dario hesitated before answering. "All right," he finally said. "But I think you're making a mistake. In this one instance, the less you know, the better off you are."

Jenna leaned back in her seat and watched the passing scenery, her happiness of a short time ago now tempered with anxiety. She had a bad feeling. It wasn't something she could explain. Just a dread deep inside that had no logic to it.

They arrived at the villa a short time later. Jenna took Jamie up to his nurse and then ran down to the stables to meet Dario. Dario led her horse out, already saddled, and eyed her skirt.

"I was afraid you wouldn't wait," she defended herself.

A corner of his mouth lifted as he pushed her hair behind her ears. "For you, I will always wait." Then he gave her a leg-up on the horse. Jenna bunched the skirt up in front of her and let the back drape over the horse.

Dario mounted his horse and looked at her. She was an unselfconscious picture of age-old equestrienne elegance.

And yet, at the same time, because she was straddling the horse rather than sitting sidesaddle, there was something of the hoyden about her. An irresistible combination. He pressed the stallion with his knees and off they went. Jenna kept up with him all the way on her spirited little mare, loving every minute of it. Oh, yes, she could get used to living here. Of one thing she was becoming more and more certain: She'd never be able to live in an apartment again. Not after this kind of freedom.

After about fifteen minutes she spotted the bullring in the distance. It was big, a lot bigger than she'd expected. A bright red wall circled the dusty ring. Ten rows of seats rose above the ring and surrounded it. Everything seemed to have a fresh coat of paint on it, giving it a clean and new look.

But as they neared it, Jenna's thoughts turned to Joachim, Dario's brother. This was probably where he had been killed. The same thing could happen to Dario.

She glanced over at him as they reined in their horses, wondering what he was thinking. He had all but forgotten about her. His attention was entirely concentrated on the ring as they rode through a narrow passage which took them right into the bullring itself. Jenna stopped her horse and watched Dario as he rode around the ring, inspecting things. She had no idea what they were, and right now she didn't think Dario was interested in explaining them to her.

There was no shade. The hot Portuguese sun beat mercilessly on the sand in the ring and reflected the heat back up. Jenna's shirt began sticking to the perspiration on her back, but she remained still, watching the man as he made his slow way around. When he finally reached her, she waited for him to speak first.

"The carpenters have done a nice job of repairing the bad spots. It looks like new." He looked at Jenna. "What do you think?"

"I think I don't like it here at all."

"Do you want to leave?"

"Yes, but I'm not going to. I'd like you to explain to me what happens in here during a bullfight."

"It's rather complicated."

She waited.

Dario relaxed back on his horse. "A Portuguese bullfight is divided into three parts. The first part involves the *cavaleiro* on horseback and his 'dance' with the bull. The second part is called the *espada,* and that involves a *torero* on foot, who fights with a cape. It is at this point that a bull has the piks placed in the hump of muscle on his neck.

Jenna's face grew instantly sympathetic for the bull. Dario shook his head. "Don't misplace your sympathies. The bull feels no pain. The entire purpose is to get the bull to carry his head a little lower. Any given bull on this ranch is capable of lifting a man and horse off the ground and tossing them ten feet through the air. It has happened. And after the fight, when the piks are removed, the bull is as good as new, even though none of the bulls will ever be used in the ring again. Bulls have long memories. That's why fights last only twenty minutes. Any longer and the bull knows what to expect. That's when he is lethal."

"You realize," Jenna told him dryly, "that this conversation is giving me absolutely no comfort whatsoever."

He just smiled at her. "The third part involves men called *forcados*. Eight *forcados* in red and green stocking caps, unprotected and unarmed, line up in Indian file, the front man facing the watching bull, provoking him to charge. When the bull does finally charge, the first man somersaults between the bull's horns, much as the ancient Minoans did. These men leap between the lowered horns and cling onto the bull's heaving, tossing head. Some of them throw themselves on the body of the bull, holding it down. This part of the fight is called the *pega*. It's probably the most popular part of the fight in Portugal.''

"I'm not going to like it."

"But this is something you must learn to live with, unless you intend taking a vacation away from Portugal every year at this time."

She tilted her head a little as she studied his strong face. "Would you consider taking one with me?"

"Is that an invitation?"

Jenna's lovely face grew serious. "Dario, I don't want you to fight."

He reached out, cupped her cheek with one hand and rubbed her mouth with his thumb. His tawny eyes held hers. "You worry too much. I've done this hundreds of times and have but a few scratches to show for my efforts."

She shook her head. "You aren't going to teach Jamie to do this, are you?"

"If he wants to learn, of course. And I should warn you now that he *will* want to. He's a Montoya. It's in the blood."

The mare stamped her hooves. Jenna straightened in the saddle. "All right. I won't say anything more about it."

"Liar," he said softly.

A dimple appeared briefly in her cheek. "I'll *try* not to say anything more about it."

Dario slapped the mare's rump. "Let's get back to the villa."

Chapter Seven

Two days later Jenna wandered outside the villa and watched the preparations for the ball that was to take place that night. An enormous barbeque pit had been set up at the far end of the grounds. Lanterns lined paths in the garden and spilled cheerfully onto the lawn. Long, white-clothed tables which would later hold mountains of food, now stood empty in the bright sun, waiting.

Basilio came up behind her and put his hands on her shoulders. "Hello, lovely lady."

Jenna smiled up at him, happy to see a friendly, familiar face. "Hello! Where have you been hiding yourself?"

He took her arm and they started walking across the lawn. "Oh, here and there. I was out of the country on business for a short time, but then so were you, I understand."

She didn't want to talk about herself. "Are you coming to the ball tonight?"

"I always do."

She glanced up at him. "And the bullfight tomorrow?"

"I *have* to go to that. I'm in it."

Jenna stopped walking, her hand on his arm. "*Et tu*, Basilio?"

He looked at her curiously. "I, too, Jenna. Though I don't fight from horseback. I'm a good rider, but not that good. I fight on foot." He touched her suddenly pale face. "You sound as though you'd been betrayed."

"Not betrayed. Just anxious. No matter how hard I try, I can't get comfortable with the idea that people I care about are going to be at the mercy of those bulls. I can't justify the danger for the thrill you men apparently get out of it." She shivered at the thought of Morte Negro. "Basilio, aren't you afraid?"

He puffed out his chest. "Afraid? Me?" He exhaled until his chest was of normal size again. "Terrified," he finished dryly.

"Then why do you do it?"

He touched his chest with his fist. "It's something in here. I don't have the words to describe it properly but there is such . . . gratification in confronting death and winning. There's nothing else like it."

"You could go for a drive in Lisbon. That's suicidal enough to be satisfying."

Basilio threw back his head and laughed. "Perhaps I'll settle for that when I'm older."

But Jenna wasn't laughing. Nothing about this was remotely amusing to her.

Basilio changed the subject. "How is Jamie liking it here?"

Then she smiled. "He loves it," she said softly. "Everyone here lavishes love and attention on him."

"And you? Are you thriving, Jenna Hart?"

She stopped and faced him. "As a matter of fact, yes. I'm growing very attached to the Ribatejo and to the people who live on the ranch."

"To some people more than others," he suggested.

"Meaning?"

"Your fondness for Dario hasn't gone unnoticed."

Her eyes met his. "You disapprove?"

"On the contrary. My sister, Elisa, was all wrong for Dario. He knew it. She knew it. They weren't happy."

The two of them stopped beneath the shade of a thick-trunked tree and sat down. Basilio held one of her hands in his and stared down at the soft palm. "Are you going to marry him?"

Jenna lifted her shoulders. "First of all, he hasn't asked me to."

"And secondly?"

Jenna paused. "And secondly, there's more to this than love, isn't there?"

"What else could there possibly be?"

"I have a life away from here, and I'm not going to give it up."

"Has anyone asked you to?"

"No—but it would inevitably come to that."

Basilio shook his head. "I don't believe you know Dario as well as you think you do."

"What if I'm not the kind of wife he wants?"

"What kind of wife is that?"

Jenna lay back on the grass, her hands behind her head. "Someone completely devoted to him, to the exclusion of anything else. The lives of Portuguese women revolve around their husbands—and that's what Dario was raised with and has lived with all these years. It's the kind of wife Elisa was. I'm not like that. I enjoy my life and my work and I don't want to give it up. No matter how much I might love a man, if I lose myself in the process, I won't be happy."

Basilio looked down at her. "I have a solution," he said quietly.

She eyed him expectantly.

"Marry me. I'll give you all the freedom you need, as long as you keep coming back to me."

"Basilio . . ." Jenna didn't know what to say.

He lifted his hand. "I'm sorry, Jenna. Ignore me. Sometimes my jokes aren't very funny."

She put a hand over her heart and closed her eyes for a moment. "Don't do that to me."

He got to his feet and hauled her up after him. "Let's go back to the villa. It's about time to start getting ready for the ball. The guests should be arriving in an hour or so.

The man standing on the small balcony outside his library watched the couple on the lawn with serious eyes. Basilio was only a year or two younger than he, but sometimes Dario felt the elder by decades. Jenna and Basilio looked good together. They enjoyed one another's company.

Dario walked thoughtfully into the library and sat down at his desk. He was treading such a fine line right now. He wanted Jenna. He had always wanted Jenna. But he loved her enough to want what was best for her, and to be brutally honest with himself, Dario just wasn't sure *he* was best for her.

A light tap on the door caught his attention. "Come."

Jenna opened the door and stepped in. A shy smile curved her mouth. "Hello."

He tossed the pen he had been holding onto the desk and relaxed back in his chair, his eyes drinking in the sight of her. "Hello."

"I know you'll be busy at the ball this evening, so I wanted to reserve a dance with you ahead of time."

"All right."

Jenna studied him for a moment. Suddenly, on an impulse, she walked over to him and kissed him lightly on the mouth.

When she pulled away, Dario lifted a black brow. "What was that for?"

"Because you looked like you needed it."

"You're a perceptive woman."

She touched the dark hair at his temples. "Not as much as I'd like to be sometimes. What's wrong?"

He put his hand over hers and sighed. "Nothing that won't work itself out in time."

Jenna knew him well enough not to probe any deeper. She got up from the corner of the desk. "I'm going to give Jamie his bath before I get ready for the ball. I guess I'll see you later." Jenna walked to the door but turned back for a moment, her eyes on Dario. She stood silently looking at him, as though trying to pierce the shield he had suddenly raised around himself, then wordlessly walked out and closed the door behind her.

Dario's eyes remained on the door for a long time after she'd gone.

In her room, Jenna could hear the people arriving at the villa. Music drifted up from the ballroom and she swayed as she fastened simple pearl earrings and then looked at herself in the mirror. She hardly recognized the woman staring back. The floor-length dress which sheathed her slender figure was of the softest, smoothest blue-green silk. Over one shoulder was a narrow strap. Her other shoulder was bare. She had braided her golden hair and wound it elegantly around her head. A few small, white flowers were artfully tucked in the braid.

Her dark lashed hazel eyes were luminous in her tanned face. Her cheeks held just a hint of pink. She applied a light coat of lipstick to her mouth, then, after taking a deep breath for courage, she headed for the stairs.

Jenna stood unnoticed at the top for a few minutes, studying the mass of humanity below. The men were all splendidly attired in their white dinner jackets. The women were lovely, elegant and bejeweled.

Suddenly Dario was at the foot of the stairs looking up at her. Wordlessly he held out his hand and waited. Her eyes on his, she held her skirt in one hand as she slowly descended. When she reached the second step from the bottom, she stopped, now eye-level with Dario. He took her hand in his and raised it to his lips, his eyes never leaving hers. He didn't have to say anything. Just the way he looked at her told her she was beautiful. And she had wanted to be. For him.

A man came up behind Dario and requested an introduction. She came down the remaining two steps and Dario very formally took her around the room and introduced her to everyone. People were all over the villa, even spilling outside onto the beautifully lighted lawns, though no one was eating yet. The night was made for dancing and laughter, and quiet conversation.

Dario got cornered by a man who wanted to talk business at about the same time that Isabella arrived and commandeered Jenna, hauling her outside the villa. "Have you seen Basilio?" she asked urgently.

"Not since this afternoon. Why?"

"Because I need to talk to him."

Jenna's eyes roamed over the faces scattered across the lawn. "Perhaps he's with Ines. Have you seen her?"

"She's here with some Spanish fellow who's in the bullfight tomorrow."

"Maybe he's still at home."

"That must be it. I'll call him there."

Jenna caught her arm before she could dash off. "What's all this about?"

"There is *the* most gorgeous fellow here. We used to know one another when we were small. I haven't seen him for years."

"And?"

"And, I want him to think I'm here with Basilio."

"You want to make this fellow jealous?"

"Exactly."

"Why?"

Isabella looked at Jenna as though she'd taken leave of her senses. "I don't want him to think I'm desperate for a date."

"It might backfire on you. If he thinks you're Basilio's girl, perhaps he won't ask you out. You *do* want this fellow to ask you out, don't you?"

"Of course. But I think I know what I'm doing. Don't worry." She rushed off to the phone.

Jenna smiled to herself and walked further out onto the lawn, rubbing her arms a little. There was a chill in the night air. She found herself moving further and further away from the people until she was alone, staring up at the star-filled sky. The music from the villa filtered softly to where she stood.

Quite suddenly, though there was no noise, she knew that Dario was approaching. She always knew when he was near. He came up behind her and put his warm hands on her shoulders, sliding them slowly down over her arms and pulling her body back against his. His warmth flowed into her. They said nothing for a long time, but it was a comfortable silence. "What are you doing way out here?" he asked against her hair.

Jenna tilted her head back. "I don't really know. I guess I was just looking for some privacy."

"Am I intruding?"

She turned in his arms and looked up at him, her hands flat against his chest. "I can't think of anyone I'd rather be private with."

He covered her right hand with his left and, with his other arm around her waist, swayed gently to the music. Jenna rested her cheek on his white jacket with a sigh and closed her eyes. She was lost and she knew it. All she wanted was to be with him. To touch him. To talk to him . . . to love him. No matter how satisfying other aspects of her life were, she could never be completely happy without Dario.

She inhaled deeply the clean scent of the soap he used. All of her senses were sharpened. Every part of her was aware of him. Aware of the heat of his body against her. Of his breath in her hair. Of the powerful shoulder beneath her cheek and the strong arm which circled her waist.

She slid her left hand under his jacket and around his

trim waist to his back. Dario pulled her closer. "Jenna," he whispered. "I wish I knew what to do."

Her hand rubbed the smooth cotton. "I thought you were never unsure about anything."

"You were wrong." He stopped moving and held Jenna slightly away from him. "What are we going to do about us?"

Her eyes searched his. "What do you want to do?"

"I want to carry you off somewhere where we can be completely alone for a year and spend the entire time getting to know each other as well as two human beings are capable of knowing one another. I want my mouth and my hands to know every inch of you. I want to know all of your thoughts and feelings and desires." He rested his mouth against her forehead. "Jenna," he whispered, "this love I feel for you is consuming me." He placed his finger under her chin and raised her face to his. "And it scares the hell out of me. I've never had to deal with anything like this before."

"If it helps any, I'm scared, too. We're so different, you and I."

Dario pulled her back into his arms. "I know."

"All we really have in common is Jamie."

"And each other."

She nodded against his chest. "Is that enough?"

"I don't know."

Suddenly Dario stepped away from her, took off his jacket and draped it around her shoulders. "Come back to the house with me. It's almost time for the *fadista*."

Jenna held her skirt out of the dew dampened grass as they walked. *"Fadista?"*

"Something you will find only in Portugal. The *fado* is our national music. A *fadista* is the woman who sings it."

As they approached the others on the lawn, a woman emerged from the house, dressed entirely in black and looking very somber. Two men accompanied her, one with a regular guitar, the other with a strange looking one. The men played alone for the first several minutes. An instant hush fell over the onlookers. Dario moved Jenna in front of him and rested his hands on her shoulders as they watched. Soon the woman in black stepped forward and struck a dramatic pose. At first Jenna listened with a critical ear. The *fadista's* voice was not classically beautiful, but there was a certain quality in it—a hauntingly lovely quality—which captured Jenna's attention and soon her heart.

Jenna didn't understand the words, but the very way the woman sang told her they were about lost love.

"Two small candles are my eyes," Dario whispered an interpretation, his mouth close to her ear. "Lighting my face with sadness. My face is marked with anguish of parting and sorrow." He kissed the tip of her ear.

Jenna looked up at him with wide eyes. "I don't want to lose you."

"There isn't much chance of that."

But Jenna knew better. There was a very *good* chance of exactly that. So many things pulled them apart and so few pushed them together.

The woman began her next song and Jenna turned to listen, but her thoughts weren't on the *fadista*. They were on her own life—and the man she loved. This had caught her by surprise. Here she was. The woman who had always been so good at making decisions. At the moment she was frightened and unsure.

As soon as the *fadista* finished her number, and before

she could start the next one, Jenna turned to Dario, taking his jacket from her shoulders and handing it to him. "I suddenly have a terrible headache. If you'll excuse me, I'd like to go to my room and rest."

Dario said nothing, but his narrowed eyes followed her into the villa.

Jenna hadn't been lying about the headache. She went straight upstairs and took two aspirin, then lay down on her bed in the darkened room staring at the ceiling. She didn't want to think about this any more. All she wanted to do was sleep. Things were going to have to work themselves out. She didn't know what to do anymore.

Jenna must have fallen asleep. When she woke, all was quiet. The party was over and the house was in darkness. She lay quietly for a time, but wide awake. There would be no more sleep for her that night and she knew it.

With a frustrated sigh, she stood up, still in her silk dress. She carelessly stripped it from her body and tossed on a pair of loose jeans and a sweater. She needed to get out for awhile.

Quietly she made her way out of the sleeping house and down to the stables where she found Arcogris dozing in her stall. She kissed the mare's nose and rested her cheek against the horse's forehead.

Within minutes she had the mare saddled and ready to go. Jenna had no plan about where she wanted to ride, but her gallop across the fields led her irresistibly to the bullring. They rode through the narrow passageway and into the ring. Jenna pulled the mare up short and just sat there quietly contemplating the place in the eerie moonlight.

Tomorrow it would be hot and dusty, crowded with people. Very big, very mean bulls would come crashing through the gate and go after whatever they saw.

The whinny of a horse sliced the air. It wasn't Arcogris. Jenna narrowed her eyes and looked around until she spotted Dario's stallion across the dark ring. She kneed Arcogris and they trotted slowly to the stallion. Dario sat on the edge of a low wall watching her. "What are you doing here?" he asked.

"I honestly don't know. What about you?"

"I always come out here the night before I do my dance with the bull."

"Would you like to be alone?"

There was a pause, then, "Not particularly." Dario pushed off the wall and mounted his horse. "It's late. I have to get some sleep. Shall we ride back together?"

Jenna wordlessly turned her horse to trot beside his.

They didn't speak for the rest of the ride. Dario seemed in a world of his own and Jenna didn't want to intrude. When they finally arrived at the stables he dismounted, then put his hands on Jenna's waist and helped her down.

For a long time he just looked at her, finally lifting his hand and pushing some stray strands of her golden hair behind her ear. "Tomorrow, after the bullfight, we will talk about us."

"What about us?"

"Tomorrow, Jenna. I haven't the energy to go into it tonight."

"Not even a hint?"

A corner of Dario's mouth lifted. "Jenna, I've come to love you too much—and I want you too badly—to go on this way."

"Meaning?" she asked tentatively.

"Meaning," he said almost in exasperation, "that we're going to have to work out a new arrangement. I want to marry you."

Jenna just looked at him.

The grooves in his cheeks deepened. "And suddenly there was silence."

"I don't know what to say."

"You could say yes."

Jenna's expressive eyes filled with the love she was feeling. "I could. I *want* to."

"But . . ."

"But I can't."

Dario's hands, still at her waist, pulled her closer. "Well, while you're considering, consider this as well." His mouth closed over hers and Jenna's body, completely without her consent, melted into his.

A stable door slammed and both of them jumped. Tomaso came slowly out of the shadows, looking embarrassed. "I saw the light," he stammered apologetically, "and came to check . . ."

Jenna smoothed her hair and stepped away from Dario. "If you'll both excuse me," there was a tremor in her voice, "I think I'll go back to the villa now." She all but broke into a run once she was out of the stables and didn't stop until she got to her room. Mechanically she took off her clothes and slipped into a simple white cotton nightgown before sliding beneath the sheets where she lay wide-eyed and sleepless, staring at the ceiling. She heard Dario come upstairs and listened to the sound of his door closing.

Jenna didn't know how long she lay there, but the next time she looked out the window, the sun was beginning to rise. And then, as though some of that light entered her own heart, she *knew*. Without any question, she knew that no matter what the obstacles, she belonged with Dario. He was the man she loved, and any problems which arose, they would handle. Her work would take her away from him, but the time they would be *together* was what counted.

Suddenly she threw the covers back and raced out of her room and into Dario's. She came to a halt beside his bed and stood looking down at him. He was on his back. The sheet covered him to his waist and his muscled torso was bare. Slowly his eyes opened and he looked right into hers.

Jenna gazed at him. "Yes," she finally said.

"There was no other answer," he said quietly.

"I know that now." He would never know what courage it took for her to say what she did next. "Make love to me."

"So that's it. You're after my body."

"I'm after all of you."

Dario lifted the sheet. Their eyes met and held as Jenna moved forward and slid under the covers. He raised himself on an elbow and looked down at her, his eyes traveling over her golden hair as it spilled across his pillow. He lifted the silky strands and let them drift through his fingers. "So often I've imagined your hair, just like this, on my pillow."

Her fingertips trailed over his carved face as he gazed into her eyes. "I don't ever want you to feel any pain because of me."

Her hand moved down the side of his neck and came to rest on his smoothly muscled chest. "Too late. Love hurts."

"I know," he said softly. "I didn't know it until I met you." He lowered his face to her hair and nuzzled her ear, breathing deeply of her light perfume. "Jenna." His voice cherished her name as his arms went around her and held her body close to his. Just held her.

Jenna closed her eyes and buried her face in his neck. The feelings that filled her were overwhelming in their intensity. How was it possible to love a man this much?

Wordlessly Dario slipped her nightgown over her head and then lay her back on the pillow. His eyes told her she was beautiful. He lay on his side next to her, his strong body against hers. He lifted himself up on an elbow and looked into her eyes. Then very slowly, as though he enjoyed the feel of her skin, his hand made its way from her shoulder to her hand. He took each of her fingers, one by one, and languorously massaged them, then made his way back over her arm to her shoulder, all the time looking into her eyes.

His fingertips trailed lightly across her throat, stopping at the vulnerable spot at its base and feeling the pulse which beat so strongly. Jenna started to say something, but Dario placed his finger against her lips. "Shhhhh," he said softly. "Close your eyes."

When she didn't, he gently touched her eyelids and moved his mouth close to her ear. "Just let yourself feel what I'm doing to you."

Jenna obeyed, a little nervous and very unsure of herself, knowing only that she didn't want him to stop.

His hand, warm and gentle, drifted over her shoulder and massaged its way down her side, sliding sensuously over her hip and thigh, then coming back up the inside of her leg and down again, and around to the outside of her hip. He put his knee between her legs as his hand traveled slowly over her flat stomach. His desire pressed against her, heightening her own awareness of what was happening to her body. The back of his hand gently brushed against her already hardened nipple causing her to gasp.

Dario kissed her earlobe. She could feel his breath, warm in her ear. "Relax," he whispered.

"Easy for you to say," she breathed as his hand once again found her breast.

His smile touched her through the half-light. Oh, he knew exactly what he was doing to her. Jenna's skin grew more and more sensitive until she wasn't aware of anything but his hands, touching her. There wasn't an inch of her that he didn't come to know intimately.

His hard, warm body half covered hers as his hand moved between her legs, bringing her to the brink again and again until she couldn't bear it any longer and he took her as completely as a man can take a woman.

The explosion that rocked Jenna left her trembling. Dario wrapped his arms around her and held her close to him. She felt him tremble as well, and loved him all the more for it.

They lay like that for a long time, then Dario laid her back on the pillow, his tawny eyes filled with a love and tenderness that brought tears to her eyes. He pushed the damp hair away from her forehead with a shaky hand. "Don't ever leave me, Jenna. I would die inside."

She traced his carved mouth with her index finger. "I love you."

Dario lay down and put his arm around Jenna, pulling her close to his side so that her cheek rested on his shoulder. Their legs were intertwined. Within minutes, Jenna's light, even breaths told the man she slept.

He rubbed his cheek against her hair and pulled her closer, then stared solemnly at the ceiling. He still had to get through the bullfight that afternoon. For the first time in his life he was worried.

He had so much to lose if he made even one mistake . . .

Chapter Eight

Jenna awoke slowly. A smile curved her mouth as she opened her eyes and found herself still in Dario's room. She could hear his shower running. A few minutes later it stopped and Dario, a towel wrapped around his waist and another thrown across the back of his neck, stepped from the steamy bathroom into the bedroom. His dark hair was still damp. Jenna's heart leaped, as she guessed it always would at the sight of him.

He walked over to the bed and looked down at her. "I love you," he said simply.

Her eyes roamed over his well-muscled chest and powerful arms, and she wanted him all over again. "Talk is cheap, buster."

Dario threw back his head and laughed, then leaned over her, a hand on either side of her head on the pillow. "So it is, Jenna." His mouth caressed hers with a slow, lingering tenderness that left her weak. Then he straightened and looked down at her. "Tomaso came to the door while you were sleeping. There is a problem with two of the horses we want to show today."

"Can't he handle it?"

"If he could, he wouldn't have bothered me."

Her lips parted softly as her eyes rested on his mouth. A muscle in his jaw worked. "And if you don't stop looking at me like that, I'll never be able to leave you."

Jenna dropped her eyes. "I'll try."

He smiled down at her for a moment before he turned and walked back into the bathroom. When he emerged a short time later, without his towels, he was completely unselfconscious, as though he was used to being without his clothes in the presence of women. Jenna just watched him. He was beautiful.

When he was dressed in his jeans and a sweater, he came back to the bed and sat down facing Jenna. "The running of the bulls will be in a few hours. Are you going?"

"What is it?"

He tucked the sheet around her. "The *campinos*—the men who herd the bulls—drive them from the pasture where they're kept to the bullring."

"Isn't that dangerous?"

"Sometimes a bull breaks away from the other bulls and oxen, but it is rare. The *campinos* on this ranch know what they're doing. And the bulls never attack when they're in a herd. Only when they get separated."

"Will you be there?"

He shook his head. "I have too much to do. Most of the men coming to the fights today are here as buyers of bulls and horses. Without them I couldn't run this ranch. They must be taken care of and shown the stock, even before the fights.''

"Then when will I see you?"

He pushed the golden hair off her forehead. "Tonight we'll meet after the bullfight and you can tell me when you plan on making an honest man of me."

Jenna gave him a mischievous smile, but it slowly faded.

"What's the matter?"

"This is going to make your grandmother very unhappy."

"She'll adjust." His eyes caressed her. "She'll have to, because we belong together, you and I. Nothing and no one can change that, ever." He kissed her forehead and rose. "I have to get going. We'll talk later and break the news to my grandmother together."

He walked to the door and opened it, but then turned and just looked at her, with her hair tousled, cheeks flushed, eyes luminous.

And then he was gone.

Jenna lay staring at the door, her teeth tugging on her lower lip. It was one thing to be in love. It was another to know that there were problems ahead of them.

And there was the bullfight that afternoon to get through.

A few hours later, a crowd of people, most of whom would later be at the bullfight, gathered along the sand track stretching between the pastures. Isabella stood next to Jenna, chattering excitedly as the gaily dressed *campinos* carrying their metal-tipped lances drove the huge black beasts right past them.

Jenna automatically took a step back. Just looking at the bulls sent her heart into her throat. Their horns were long and needle-sharp. She had been doing some reading lately and knew that those horns could pierce bone as though it were paper.

And yet, she had to admit, the bulls were beautiful in a terrible kind of way—full of dignity, and as innocent of civilization as circumstances would allow them to be.

In a cloud of dust, the bulls got safely past the crowd. Some of the people followed along behind, but Jenna went back to the house. That gnawing dread returned to eat at her for the rest of the afternoon.

Isabella hammered at her bedroom door. "Come on, Jenna. We have to leave now or we'll be late."

Jenna opened the door. "I'm ready. Are we going to the ring on horseback?"

Isabella shook her dark head as she and Jenna ran down the steps. "It's too late. We'll have to take my car."

A small, white convertible was parked and waiting. The two climbed in and before Jenna had even closed her door, Isabella had taken off. They bumped along the same road the bulls had taken earlier that morning. Jenna squinted into the distance. At five o'clock in the evening, the Portuguese sun was still hot and bright. They arrived in a few minutes. Isabella pulled alongside dozens of other cars, enveloping them in a swirl of choking dust.

Without even bothering to take the keys out of the ignition, she leaped out of the car and raced for the ring, with Jenna following closely behind. As they climbed through the filled seats, Isabella grabbed Jenna's hand and tugged her along to the shady side of the ring where seats had been saved for them.

The minute they were seated, Isabella swore softly under her breath.

"What's the matter?"

"We missed the opening parade. That's where the *cavaleiros*—the fighters on horseback—and the others walk around the ring. If this were in Lisbon, they would be wearing the elaborate costumes of the sixteenth century, but here they will be wearing a simple black short-jacketed suit and flat-brimmed hat. Dario hates all that plummage, as he calls it. He much prefers the simplicity of the small fights in the Ribatejo.

A small breeze lifted Jenna's hair from the back of her hot neck. "Who fights first?"

"The *cavaleiros*. There are two, Dario and another man, but who goes first depends upon the luck of the draw."

Jenna waited, her hands clasped tightly in her lap, her eyes on the doorway where the first fighter would emerge.

Horse and rider came out of the dark tunnel and into the sunlight. Jenna's heart leaped. It was Dario, dressed as Isabella had said he would be, with a plain white shirt beneath the black jacket.

Isabella leaned over. "Normally," she explained, "he would be carrying short, narrow piks which he would place in the lump of muscle on the bull's neck during the passes, but Dario doesn't like to do that. He prefers to fight the bull without taking away any of the bull's advantages."

Dario, straight in his saddle, rode halfway around the ring and stopped. Horse and rider were perfectly still as they waited.

The toril gate suddenly lifted and a black bull exploded

into the ring. He stopped and stood as menacingly still as Dario as he looked around the ring, his eyes adjusting to the light. Dario and his horse moved. The lump of muscle on the bull's neck raised as he spotted his target.

Without any warning at all, and with a burst of speed Jenna would never have believed possible, the bull charged Dario. Her heart stopped. Dario just sat there, and Jenna couldn't even scream at him to get out of the way. No sound would come out. Then, when she thought it was all over, Dario, with a barely perceptible movement, danced the stallion out of the furious bull's way. The lethal horns missed them by inches. The crowd screamed it's approval and Jenna breathed again.

The bull wheeled and turned, churning up dust. Enraged, he again sighted the man and the horse and charged, and again Dario waited until the last minute before dancing the horse out of the way.

Jenna's confidence in Dario grew to the point where she could even relax a little as she watched. It was beautiful. Horribly beautiful. She was fascinated.

Isabella touched her arm. "You'll like the next part. This is where he would ordinarily place the piks in the bull, but in his case, he goes through all the motions. I think it's more exciting this way because the bull still has all of his strength."

Jenna waited. Dario raised his arms high over his head so that he was controlling the horse entirely with his legs. Then he went on the offensive. Simultaneously, from opposite ends of the ring, man and bull charged one another. She thought they were going to collide. The bull looked like a train on a track, charging straight down the rails, as did Dario and his horse. At the very last moment, though, the stallion veered to the left, just enough to allow the bull to thunder harmlessly past as Dario deftly leaned over in the saddle and touched the bull as he went by. Again the crowd roared its approval.

The black beast turned quickly, his sides heaving with fury at another missed opportunity. Dario's teeth flashed white in his dark face, obviously enjoying the encounter. Immediately the bull charged again, and again and again, and each time Dario danced his horse out of the way, using only his legs. Jenna was on the edge of her seat, her knuckles white as she clasped her hands harder and harder.

After twenty minutes, the *campinos* rode into the ring with some oxen and escorted the bull out. The crowd roared its approval. The stallion, with Dario still on his back, took an elegant bow. When they straightened, Dario looked up and right into Jenna's eyes. A corner of his mouth lifted as he inclined his head toward her and then left the ring.

Jenna sat back in her seat and took a real breath for the first time in minutes. It was over. He was all right.

The next *cavaleiro* did a nice job, but somehow it didn't look as dangerous as it had when Dario was doing it. The crowd's restrained applause when he finished told her they felt the same.

Then it was Basilio's turn. He came out on foot, looking very tall and elegant. He dragged his yellow and magenta cape across the sand a few times, and then waited, his eyes on the toril gate.

"Why did he do that?"

Isabella glanced over at her. "Drag his cape?"

Jenna nodded.

"There is some wind. Before he came out he poured water on his cape to make it heavy and then dragged it in the sand to make it even heavier. This makes it less likely that a sudden gust will catch the cape and blow it toward the man."

"What would happen if it did?"

Isabella's eyes returned to the ring. "The bull would follow it into the man."

Jenna sat in silence for a moment, then touched Isabella's arm. "I don't think my heart can take another twenty minutes of this."

The Portuguese woman smiled. "You get used to it, believe me. And I've seen people killed."

Suddenly the gate went up and a bull shot into the ring as though fired from a gun. His hot eyes searched for something to attack. Basilio visibly paled. Something was wrong.

On the first charge the bull hooked into the cape and moved his huge head as though searching for the man. Isabella gasped. "This is not a fresh bull! It has been worked before!"

Jenna stared into the ring. "How can you tell?"

"He knows the man is the enemy, not the cape. Bulls are smart. Once they've been worked they never forget it."

"But this bull is right off the range. How could that happen?"

"Young would-be matadors steal into the pastures at night and work the bulls. Sometimes they get caught. Sometimes not."

Jenna watched more closely. The creature certainly seemed to know what he was doing. After the first charge he hauled up short and turned. Then he stood there, assessing the situation with a calm that was chilling.

Dario apparently recognized that there was a problem as well because he stood to the side, his cape at the ready to help if the need arose.

Basilio stood his ground as the bull once again hooked into the cape. A hush fell over the crowd. They knew the man in the ring was in trouble and wanted nothing to interrupt his concentration.

In the next rush, the bull's flank bumped him, knocking him to the ground. He was hurt and had trouble getting up. Isabella and Jenna both sucked in their breath as the bull wheeled around, ready to attack the helpless man.

"Hoi! Toiro!" Dario's voice cut across the ring. With lightning speed, the bull wheeled in a flurry of hooves to confront this new enemy. Jenna's heart caught in her throat at the sight of him standing there so straight and tall with nothing more than a scrap of cloth to protect him from the anger of the bull. Dario moved toward him, calling to him. Goading him. Anything to get him away from Basilio until the horsemen got there.

The bull suddenly shot forward. Dario stopped walking and took up his stance, waiting. The bull roared past with only inches to spare as Dario flicked the cape with his wrist.

Jenna wanted to close her eyes as the bull wheeled and charged again and again, but she couldn't. She was afraid something would happen to Dario if she did.

He stayed out there and worked the bull with a grace and courage that was awesome to behold while some other men ran into the ring to help Basilio out. The horrible thing was so intent on Dario, he didn't even glance at the activity there.

The breeze picked up. Jenna felt it in her hair. Dario's yellow and magenta cape gently flapped.

Isabella looked grim. "He has had no time to dampen his cape."

It came upon Jenna with quiet horror that this was it. Slowly she got to her feet, her eyes burning as she refused to even blink. The next sixty seconds were in slow motion. The bull charged. For a moment it appeared as though it would pass by the man, but then, without warning, a gust of wind blew the cape toward Dario's legs. The bull followed it. His enormous head smashed into Dario, lifting him off the ground and throwing him over his massive shoulders as though he were nothing more than a rag doll.

Jenna couldn't even scream as she watched. Dario lay in the ring on his back, motionless. The bull wheeled, still in a rage, and started for him again, to finish what he had started. But suddenly two mounted *campinos* rode into the ring with several oxen and got the bull under control and out of the ring.

Adrenalin surged into Jenna's bloodstream. She raced through the crowd and into the ring, pushing herself past a growing circle of people who surrounded Dario. She dropped onto her knees beside him. He was so still!

Tomaso was there. She looked up at him, the thing she feared most in her eyes. He shook his head and kneeled beside her. "He is not dead, but badly injured. We must get him to a hospital."

She looked back at the man she loved, afraid to touch him for fear of hurting him further. With a shaking, tentative hand, she reached out and pushed the dark hair from his forehead. She leaned forward, her mouth close to his ear. "Dario?"

He didn't answer.

She swallowed and dashed at a hot tear which fell down her cheek. "Don't you dare leave me again," she whispered. "Please."

Tomaso put his hands on her shoulders and lifted her away from Dario when several men with a stretcher ran up. Very carefully they lifted him onto it, trying not to jar him, and walked toward a waiting truck. Jenna would have followed, but Tomaso stopped her. "Isabella brought a car. We'll go in that."

"What happened to Basilio?" she asked dully.

"He is already on his way to the hospital. I think his leg is broken."

Jenna's damp eyes found Isabella staring dolefully after Dario's disappearing stretcher. Jenna walked over to her and gave her a hug. This was the second brother she had seen hurt here. The first hadn't made it. "He'll be fine. You'll see." Jenna's words sounded more confident than she felt. "Tomaso is going to drive us to the hospital."

Isabella wordlessly followed Jenna to the car and climbed into the back seat. They closely tailed the truck carrying Dario for the twenty-minute drive to the small hospital. Jenna jumped out of the car the moment it stopped and ran over to the truck. Dario was conscious, but obviously in a great deal of pain. Sweat beaded his forehead as the men lifted him down and carried him into the hospital. Jenna's eyes met his. He winked at her just before they carried him through the doors, and then she was alone.

Tomaso touched her shoulder and she jumped. "Let's wait inside."

Isabella took Jenna's hand in hers and they walked into

the hospital like that. The waiting room was just down the corridor. Tomaso excused himself while the two women sat on a long couch in silence and waited.

It seemed like hours before a young doctor walked into the room and looked at them. "Jenna Hart?"

Jenna stood, waiting for the worst.

"Come with me please."

She glanced at Isabella with dark hazel eyes. Isabella pressed Jenna's hand and then held it against her cheek for a moment.

She followed the doctor down the corridor. "What's going on? Is it serious?"

"Yes, it's serious. And he needs surgery. But first he insists on seeing you."

He opened a large door and ushered her in, then closed it behind her and left. Dario lay on a table. His clothes had been cut off him and lay in a heap off to one side. He was covered with a clean, white sheet up to his waist. His stomach was badly bruised. His eyes opened into hers. "Hello."

She took his hand in hers and let a little of her strength flow into him. "Hi."

"We don't have much time, Jenna, so I'll get right to the point. I want you to marry me."

Jenna blinked at the unexpectedness of his words. "But I already said yes."

"I mean I want you to marry me now, before the surgery. Tomaso is bringing a priest."

She started to say something—she didn't know what—but Dario interrupted. "Jenna, there are two very good reasons. The adoption papers for Jamie haven't been signed yet. If I don't make it through this surgery, he could end up with nothing. But with you as my wife, you will automatically inherit everything and can in turn see that Jamie gets what is rightfully his when he comes of age. I know I can trust you to do this.''

''And the second reason?''

Tawny eyes gazed into hazel. ''Even now, you could be carrying my child. I want you to be protected. I want the child to have my name.'' He paused. ''There's a very good chance I'm not going to survive the surgery.'' He turned his head away from her a little. ''Perhaps that would be best.''

Jenna stared at Dario, wondering if she'd heard correctly, but there was no more time for talking. Tomaso arrived with the priest. All legalities had been pushed through because of the circumstances. Dario looked up at her. ''Well, my Jenna, what's your decision?''

Jenna looked into his eyes. ''There's no decision to make.'' Then she turned to the priest and waited. He glanced at Dario, then began the ceremony, in both English and Portuguese.

When it was finished, Jenna leaned over and kissed Dario. ''I've made an honest man of you,'' she said softly. ''Now don't *you* make a widow of me.''

He touched her cheek. ''I'm sorry there's no ring.''

''I don't need a ring. All I need is you.''

The doctor came in. ''Everyone has to leave now.''

Tomaso walked behind her and literally moved her away from Dario and through the door to the corridor. ''Go back to Isabella. I will wait here.''

She turned her stricken eyes on him. ''I don't want to leave him.''

''Senhora Montoya,'' he said firmly, ''you can't help

your husband right now. He is on his own. It will do him no good to see you standing here crying.''

Jenna reached up and touched her damp cheek. She hadn't even known. Wordlessly she turned and walked back to Isabella. She sat down next to the Portuguese woman and took her hand. ''He's going into surgery. From what I can gather, he has an injury to his spinal cord.''

Isabella closed her eyes and said something in Portuguese. They sat in silence after that and waited.

Hours passed. Jenna looked up sharply at the sound of someone coming down the corridor. Basilio limped in on crutches, one leg in a cast. His face was pale as he looked at the two women. ''I'm so sorry.''

Isabella ran over and threw her arms around him. Jenna didn't have the energy. She just looked at him. ''It wasn't your fault.''

''It was! I should have gotten out of the ring the moment I realized the bull had been worked, but no, I had to be a hero and stick it out. If I hadn't, Dario wouldn't be in surgery at this moment.''

''Don't, Basilio,'' she said tiredly. ''It doesn't matter now. It's done.''

Isabella helped him into the chair next to Jenna and then sat on his other side, holding his hand. He smiled wanly at Isabella, but his eyes kept wandering to Jenna's pale profile.

Finally Jenna turned her head. She had forgotten he was there. She didn't seem to be able to concentrate on anything. ''Is your leg broken?''

''In two places. I'll be in this thing,'' he nodded toward the cast, ''for six weeks.''

"Shouldn't you be resting?"

"I couldn't. I wanted to be here with the two of you. Have you heard anything?"

Jenna shook her head and went back to staring blankly into space.

When the doctor finally did enter the waiting room, Jenna stood up like a prisoner awaiting sentencing. She asked no questions. She just looked at him.

He took her hand and sat down with her. His eyes held hers. "Your husband made it through the surgery."

Jenna breathed again. Both Isabella and Basilio started at the mention of Dario as her husband.

"He is going to have a long recovery, though," the doctor continued. "And there is a very good possibility that he will never walk again."

Jenna heard his words. Now she knew what Dario had meant by the statement he had made before going into surgery. But over and over again in her mind she kept repeating that he was alive. He made it. Losing him was the one thing she didn't think she could deal with.

They would get through this.

"When can I see him?"

"He's still in the recovery room. He'll be there for the rest of the night. It's not common practice, but if you'd like to sit with him for awhile, I think it can be arranged."

For the first time, a grateful smile touched her mouth. "Thank you."

He turned to Isabella. "And I would ask that you take this gentleman home," he said of Basilio. "He needs to get some rest."

Isabella nodded, still clutching Basilio's hand. "I will. Right away."

Jenna followed the doctor to the recovery room. He

made her put a sterile gown over her clothes, and then he led her across the room to Dario's bed. His left arm had tubes in it, so she went to the right side of the bed and took his hand in hers and held it against her cheek. He looked so pale. A frown creased his forehead, even in his drugged sleep.

The doctor pushed a chair behind her and with his hands on her shoulders, gently lowered her into it. "I'll come back for you in an hour."

She nodded, but her eyes never left Dario. With indescribable tenderness she pushed his dark hair away from his forehead. "I'm here," she said softly. "And I love you. Everything will be all right."

He was still. It was almost forty minutes before his eyelids fluttered a little and then finally opened. Jenna leaned over him as he tried to focus. "Jenna?" he asked.

"I'm right here."

His fingers weakly gripped her hand. "I recognized your perfume." His gaze came to rest on her tired face. "Hello."

A tremulous smile touched her mouth. "Hello."

"How am I doing?"

She touched his cheek. "You're here. That's all that matters."

He seemed to know instinctively from her words that what he had feared had happened. His jaw grew taut and he turned his head away from her. "Damn."

She turned his face back to her and forced him to look at her. "Don't talk. Don't think. Just rest," she whispered.

His tawny eyes moved over her face with an intensity that left her shaken. "Go home, Jenna," he finally said. "You look tired."

"I'd rather stay with you."

"Please. I don't have the strength to argue. Just do as I ask." He looked at her for a moment longer and then slowly closed his eyes.

Jenna stayed with him until the doctor came back for her, but then she had to leave. Faithful, caring Tomaso awaited her in the corridor. Without saying a word, he took her home.

Chapter Nine

Contrary to her expectations, Jenna slept soundly that night. And the next morning she was at the hospital early. Dario had been moved into a private room. When she walked in he turned his head and looked at her, but he had no reaction. She could have been a stranger.

Jenna's smile faded. "Good morning."

"What are you doing here?"

There was something in his voice that stopped her where she was. "I thought you might like some company. I wanted to be with you."

He turned his head away from her and stared out of the window next to his bed. "Go home, Jenna."

"Dario . . ."

"I don't want any company today, or tomorrow, or the day after that, all right? I just want to be left alone."

"But perhaps I can help . . ."

He cut her off again. Tawny eyes bored into her. "I don't want your help. I don't want your pity and I don't want your mothering."

She just stood there feeling helpless and hurt.

Dario's jaw grew taut as he looked at her expressive face, but it didn't change anything. "I'm tired, Jenna."

She backed away from him, and with a final look, turned and left. Dario looked back out the window, his tawny eyes hollow, his fists clenched by his sides.

Two days after the accident, Dario and Isabella's grandmother died without ever knowing that her grandson had married Jenna. Things at the villa were shrouded in quiet.

Over a month passed before she saw Dario again. He wouldn't allow her to come to the hospital. He wanted nothing to do with her.

This morning, as the sun spilled through her bedroom windows, Jenna paced. Today he was coming home. She didn't know what to expect. Her stomach was tied in knots. She had changed clothes three times, wanting to look just right for him.

When she heard a car pull to a stop in front of the villa, she dashed to the window and leaned out to look. It was Tomaso! And Dario was in the car with him. With a leap of her heart, she ran to her mirror and nervously smoothed her immaculate white dress and brushed her hair. She walked to the bedroom door, her hand poised over the knob, but suddenly she stopped, her hand arrested in midair, and closed her eyes. She took a deep breath and exhaled, straightened her shoulders and then slowly made her way downstairs.

The foyer was deserted. Jenna walked to the front door

and opened it. Dario sat there in his wheelchair with Tomaso behind him. He looked up and into her hazel eyes and it was as though a mask suddenly fell into place. She wanted to throw her arms around him so badly that she had to clasp her fingers behind her back to keep from doing it. "Hello, Dario," she managed finally.

He inclined his dark head—and then ignored her. Hurt filled her eyes as he spoke to Tomaso in Portuguese and then wheeled himself into the library.

Tomaso put his hand comfortingly on her shoulder. "It is a difficult time for him, Senhora. Be patient."

Isabella, unaware of the undercurrents, came running down the steps. "Did I hear my brother?"

Jenna swallowed and cleared her throat. "He's in the library." Then she walked past Isabella with all the dignity she possessed and went to her room.

Isabella's smile faded, to be replaced with a frown as she turned around and followed Jenna, unceremoniously pushing the door open and walking in. "What's going on here? My brother just arrives and you barricade yourself in your room."

"He doesn't want me right now, Bella."

"Nonsense."

Jenna turned away from the window to face her. "He refused to see me the entire time he was at the hospital." Tears filled her eyes. "He's shut me out, Bella. What am I supposed to do?"

Isabella walked over to Jenna and put her arm around her shoulders. "Don't give up on him. You're his wife. He needs you, whether he wants to admit it or not. He'll come around."

"He seems to want to hurt me."

"He's angry right now. He's lashing out at everyone.

Ignore it and know that it isn't you he hates. It's himself and what this accident has done to him."

"I understand that, but it doesn't make it any easier."

"I know. But the important thing right now is Dario. You come back downstairs with me and we'll face him together."

Jenna wrapped her arms around herself and walked back to the window. "You go ahead. I'll follow in a few minutes."

"You're sure?"

"I'm a woman of my word." She inclined her head toward the door. "Go ahead. I'm sure he's wondering what's keeping you."

Isabella hesitated, but only for a moment. When the door had closed behind the Portuguese woman, Jenna's shoulders slumped forward. She felt so helpless. She stood there for several minutes, pulling herself together, then walked to her mirror and studied the woman staring back at her. She was a sorry sight. Taking a deep breath, she straightened her shoulders and went to the library.

Dario looked up when Jenna stepped in. Isabella patted the couch next to her. "Come sit here, Jenna."

"No." Dario's voice cut through the room. "I'd like to be alone for awhile."

Isabella started to rise, but Jenna waved her back to her seat. "Please," she said calmly, "don't send your sister away on my account. I'm sorry to have disturbed you." She started for the door, but stopped and turned, looking straight into Dario's eyes. "I'm glad you're home," she told him softly, and then left before the tears started.

She didn't see the look of pain that crossed his face at her words.

She walked quickly down the hall and straight into

Basilio's chest. One arm supported a crutch, but his free arm went around her. "Hey, pretty lady," he teased, "there's no need to throw yourself at me." Then he got a look at her face and his smile faded. "What's the matter, Jenna?"

She tiredly rubbed her forehead. "It's nothing, Basilio. If you're looking for Isabella and Dario, they're in the library."

"I found who I'm looking for. Let's go for a walk."

"I really don't think . . ."

"Come on. You'll feel better."

She smiled despite herself. "Yes, doctor."

He led her out to the gardens and lowered himself onto a cushioned wooden bench, patting the place next to him. Jenna sat down with a tired sigh. "So what's going on?" he asked.

She lifted her shoulders in a delicate shrug. "The same thing as before. He doesn't want to see me."

"Jenna . . ." He put his hand under her chin and turned her face toward his. "He loves you."

"Then why is he doing this?" Her voice cracked on the words.

Basilio ran his fingers through his unruly hair. "You know, since all this happened, Isabella and I have grown very . . . close."

"I know."

"Well," he said quietly, "if the situation were reversed and I were the one in the wheelchair, it would kill me to look at Bella, knowing that nothing between us could ever be the same. And it would be *because* I love her."

Jenna leaned her elbows on her legs and held her face in her hands. "I understand that, but it doesn't matter to me. All I want is *him*."

"Have you told him?"

"When would I have the chance? I can't get within ten feet of him without being ordered to leave."

"He's home now. You'll have more of a chance to get close to him again. Just don't give up on him."

"Of course I won't give up on him. He's my husband."

"So he is."

Jenna stared at Basilio for a long moment, then she smiled. "You're a good friend. Thank you." With a sigh that started at her toes, she put her head on his shoulder. Basilio's arm went around her and gave her an affectionate squeeze.

"You're welcome, lovely lady. And if things get a little rough in the weeks to come, escape to me. Talking helps."

Neither of them saw the man watching them from the library, his jaw clenched at his utter helplessness.

The days passed. Jenna occupied herself with Jamie and her work. Most afternoons she took the baby to the garden and sat drawing while he played. Dario was coolly civil to her. No more. No less. But there was an anger in him. She could feel it when they happened to be in the same room together. He wasn't angry with her, though he seemed to focus it on her. He was just *angry*. He even detached himself from Jamie.

A lift was installed on the staircase so he could get himself up and down without help. He wanted to be completely independent, and he was succeeding.

One afternoon she was walking past the library and heard furniture crashing. Panicked, she ran in and found Dario standing, his entire weight supported by his arms as he leaned on his desk. A lamp had crashed to the floor. He looked up and their eyes met. She wanted desperately to help him, but knew enough to simply back out of the room and close the door behind her.

Most of his time was spent in his library where she could hear his typewriter until the wee hours of the morning.

This was one of those mornings. Jenna picked her watch up off the end table and squinted at the dial. Two-thirty. With a sigh she flopped back onto her pillow and stared at the ceiling. This was getting her nowhere.

After a few more minutes, she got up and put on her long, white robe and padded barefoot down to the kitchen. She made two cups of cocoa and carried them to the library. When she entered, Dario, at his desk, looked up. He watched in silence as she set one of the cups on the desk for him and then curled up in a chair across from him, resting her own cup on her knee. She inclined her head toward his cocoa. "You're welcome."

He remained silent, his tawny eyes on her.

"I couldn't sleep," she explained as though they were carrying on a perfectly normal conversation. "I heard you typing so I thought I'd keep you company for awhile."

He leaned back in his chair. "It's just as well. We need to talk."

Now it was Jenna's turn to study the man she loved in silence. "I'm not going to like this conversation, am I?" she finally asked.

"I want you to go back to Chicago. You can take Jamie with you. I won't make any claim on him, though I'd like to see him once in awhile."

She set her cup on the desk. "I was right. I'm not going to like this at all."

"You're a fool if you don't get out."

Jenna didn't even blink. "Yes, I suppose I am—if being a fool means wanting to stay with a man who won't have anything to do with me."

"You're letting pity blind you, Jenna."

She looked at him in astonishment. "Pity! Is that what you think?"

"I can see it in your eyes every time you look at me."

Jenna moved next to him and knelt by his wheelchair, her eyes raised to his. "What you see is a woman whose love is unwavering, even though you have hurt me again and again since the accident. But I keep coming back for more because I know one of these days you're going to realize that you still love me and that when all is said and done, nothing is more important than that."

He reached out to touch her cheek.

Jenna closed her eyes and covered his hand with hers. "Don't shut me out any more, Dario. Let me back into your life."

"I can't," he whispered harshly.

"Dario . . ."

He pulled his hand away from her. "Go back to bed, Jenna. And tomorrow think about going back to Chicago and your life there."

"My life is here because you're here. My work is in Chicago."

"I want our marriage annulled."

Jenna sat back on her heels. "You what?"

"You heard me."

"You can't mean it."

"If you'll recall the reasons for our marriage, you'll see that it isn't necessary any more. I made it through the surgery."

"What I recall is the night before our marriage. You loved me then, or you could never have made love to me the way you did."

He was unimpressed. "Circumstances have changed things since then."

"Not for me."

"Especially for you. My God, Jenna, you are a passionate woman. Look at me." He took her face in his hands. "Really look at me. Is this what you want to be stuck with for the rest of your life? You're only twenty-four years old."

A sudden fury was unleashed in Jenna. She straightened abruptly and moved away from him, placing the desk between the two of them. Her hazel eyes darkened almost to black. She finally understood what this was all about. He felt that the honorable thing to do was give her her freedom, whether she wanted it or not.

"You and your damned honor!" she yelled at him. "How *dare* you. The only man I've ever been passionate about—or with—is you. I don't want anyone else. I never have. And then to presume that the only thing that holds us together is sex is insulting and wrong. My God, Dario, I love you. Doesn't that count for anything? I deserve better than that from you." Infuriated, she picked up her empty cup and threw it against the wall and then stood there staring at the broken pieces, her chest still heaving with emotion. Silence hung heavily in the room. Dario watched her without expression as the realization of what she had done dawned on her. She raised both hands to rub her aching temples. "God, I've never thrown anything in my life," she said tightly before kneeling on the carpeting to pick up the pieces.

He watched in silence as she dropped the china into his wastebasket. "I haven't changed my mind," he finally told her.

Her eyes met his. "Neither have I."

He shook his dark head. "Where is your pride, Jenna? I don't love you. I don't want you in my life, and yet you stubbornly refuse to leave."

Quick tears stung Jenna's eyes at his cruelty, but she blinked them back. "Good night, Dario."

His gaze followed her out the door. He heard her break into a run down the tiled hall and climb the stairs. He heard her door shut. Slowly he bent his head and said her name in an anguished whisper.

During the days that followed the confrontation in the library, Jenna spent almost all of her time with Jamie or riding Arcogris. It was lonely in the villa. Ines had gone back to France, and Isabella and Basilio were so wrapped up in each other that the rest of the world hardly existed for them. Jenna liked watching them exchanging secret glances and touching each other's hands.

Dario was living more and more at his apartment in Lisbon, and when he was at the villa, he made sure he was as unpleasant as possible to Jenna. Her conviction that she was doing the right thing faltered. Her belief that he still loved her, despite what he said to the contrary, suffered blow after blow, and she wasn't bouncing back from them the way she had at first.

One night Jenna had a nightmare. Suddenly she was sitting straight up in bed, perspiration beading her forehead. An almost overwhelming sadness filled her, but she couldn't remember anything about the dream. She wrapped her arms around her knees and rocked herself, dashing every few minutes at the tears which came unbidden to her eyes.

Without thinking, she rose and walked down the hall to Dario's room. He was in Lisbon. She knew that. His room was in darkness. She walked to the bed and climbed beneath the sheets, taking one of his pillows and hugging it tightly against her, burying her tearstained face in its coolness. She could smell his aftershave. Suddenly the sobs she had held back for so long broke through the barrier and racked her slender body.

Dario came in the front door with Tomaso behind him, carrying a suitcase. Dario moved his wheelchair onto the lift and took the suitcase on his lap. "Go on to bed now, Tomaso," he told the man as he pushed a button and started up the stairs. "It's late."

When Dario got to the top, he wearily wheeled himself to his bedroom. The door was ajar. He stopped at a sound coming from inside and listened, then lowered his head, his jaw taut, as he realized what it was. After a moment he lifted his hand to push the door further open, wanting to comfort her, but it fell back into his lap. He was the cause. He couldn't be the solution. So he sat there, waiting, until Jenna's sobs grew softer and finally stopped altogether and only hiccoughs punctuated her breathing.

Then he turned and went back downstairs.

When Jenna awoke the next morning she was still in Dario's room. She was as tired as though she hadn't been to bed at all, but she had made a decision.

With a heavy heart, she went back to her own room and into her bathroom where she took a washcloth, soaked it in cold water and held it against her face. Then she dressed in

loose jeans and a short-sleeved white shirt and went
downstairs for breakfast.

Her steps faltered at the sight of Dario already seated at
the table reading his newspaper. She sat down across from
him and spread a napkin on her lap. "I didn't know you
were back," she said quietly.

He looked at her over the top of the paper and felt his
heart soften at her pale, tired face. "I know."

"I've decided that Jamie and I will leave tomorrow."

The muscle in his jaw worked. "I see."

Her eyes met his. "This is what you've wanted for
months. I expected a little more enthusiasm."

"I'm sorry you're disappointed."

A servant brought her an egg and some bacon, and a
silence fell between them until the woman had gone. "Are
you going back to Chicago?" Dario asked.

"Naturally. Not to the apartment, though. I'm going to
buy a house with some property for Jamie to play on."

"I'll make sure my attorney sends you monthly checks
for Jamie's support."

"Thank you." She took a deep breath, but even that
was an effort. "This is a good time for me to go.
Hart-Windom is having it's next showing in six weeks and
Christy is already beginning to panic."

"I guess she can't handle the company without you
after all."

"I guess not." She put her napkin back on the table and
pushed her untouched plate away.

"You should eat something. You're getting too thin."

"Whether I eat or not really isn't any of your business
now, is it?" There was no bitterness; just a calm matter-
of-factness.

"Jenna . . ."

She lifted her hand as she moved her chair back and rose. "Please, Dario, no polite, sentimental platitudes. I can't handle it." Her lower lip quivered as she looked at him, and again the man had to force his hands to stay in his lap instead of reaching for her. This was the right thing to do.

"I still love you," she went on. "Nothing will ever change that, but I can't live like this any longer. I'm unhappy all the time, and that's what Jamie sees. It isn't good for him." She swallowed. "I'll send you pictures of him and keep you up on what he's doing."

"Thank you."

"Goodbye."

"Goodbye, Jenna."

Straightening her shoulders, she turned from Dario and walked down to the stables to say goodbye to Arcogris.

Dario's dark tawny eyes followed her all the way to the stables. When she disappeared from sight, he pushed his own untouched plate away and wheeled himself back into the house.

Jenna didn't see Dario for the rest of the day. He didn't show up for dinner, and so she went to bed, ready to leave with Jamie first thing in the morning.

Sleep came as soon as her head touched the pillow, but it was short-lived. Thunder, which had been rumbling in the distance for hours, finally reached the ranch. Lightning was so close it lit the room as though it were daylight and the thunder cracked and roared through the pastures.

She lay there, her hands behind her head, looking toward the window. Suddenly there was a flash of light-

ning and a simultaneous, deafening crash that brought her
to her feet and sent her running to the window. Lightning
had hit the stables and flames were shooting into the air.

She quickly slipped her arms into her robe and ran into
the hall. Dario had come out of his room. "What's going
on?"

"The stables were hit."

He wheeled his chair onto the lift, his face suddenly
hard. "There must be twenty horses in there."

Jenna walked down the stairs beside him. When they
got to the bottom, she wheeled him off the lift and out the
door. The men who worked and lived on the ranch were
already running toward the stables.

She pushed Dario over the lawn as sheets of rain soaked
them and lightning fingered its way through the skies
around them. The thought of Arcogris quickened her
steps. By the time they got there, the fire had really
grabbed hold and was burning out of control. Men were
racing around, throwing mud and water onto the flames. A
dozen horses were milling around. Jenna urgently checked
each of them, but Arcogris was nowhere to be found. The
frantic whinnying of the horses still in the stables filled her
with horror, and nobody was doing anything about it. The
flames had cut off half of the entrance to the stables. It
would be dangerous to go in there . . .

But the thought of Arcogris and all those other poor
horses took precedence over her fear. Taking off her wet
robe, she held it over her head and ran into the burning
building. Ignoring Dario's shouts at her to come back, she
carefully picked her way over the fallen rafters.

Thick smoke filled the building, burning her eyes and
her lungs. She tried to squint through it as she made her
way to the horses she could hear. For the first time she

realized just how long the stables were. Nearly a city block. She found Arcogris about halfway down.

She stroked the little mare in an effort to calm her, then went to work on the other hysterical horses. Getting them out without getting kicked in the process was tricky, but one by one they took off like shots and made it to safety.

Then it was Jenna's turn. She started picking her way back to the entrance. Chunks of steaming, blackened wood were falling around her. She was beginning to feel lightheaded from all the smoke.

A large rafter, still burning, fell in front of her, showering her with sparks and blocking her path. She couldn't get over it or around it. There wasn't anything she could do.

She swayed. A wave of weakness washed over her. Her knees buckled and she couldn't get back up. "Oh, damn," she whispered.

"Jenna!" Dario's voice cut through her faintness.

"I can't get out!" she called back. "There's fire behind me and fallen rafters in front of me. I can't get over them."

More burning wood fell around her. She was too weak to do anything about it as the smoke filled her lungs. "I don't want to die this way," she moaned softly as she fainted.

Dario found her, though it wasn't easy through the smoke. Tomaso stood by his side, knowing that they hadn't much time before this entire side of the stables was engulfed in flames. The smoke made their eyes water. Dario shook his head. "We need more help, Tomaso. Go out and bring back some more men."

"But . . ."

"Hurry up," he ordered roughly.

The flames got nearer and nearer. The rain outside wasn't helping to put them out, but the winds from the storm were fanning them as they swirled down through a gaping black hole in the roof. Another rafter fell, narrowly missing Dario, but it hit the other rafters and made an opening large enough for a man to crawl through.

Tomaso hadn't returned. Dario could still see Jenna's outline on the floor through the smoke. He had to get her out. He caused his wheelchair to fall over so that he was on the ground. Using his upper body strength, he pulled himself through the opening in the rafters until he got to Jenna. She was unmoving. He couldn't rouse her, which meant that he had to get her through the opening on his own.

He placed one arm beneath her breasts and pulled, while dragging himself backward with his other arm. He could have screamed at the uselessness of his legs.

He got himself through, and Jenna part of the way, but then her body got stuck on something. He couldn't budge her. He needed something on which to brace himself so he would have the leverage to pull her. There was another rafter by his left foot. He literally willed that foot to move six inches so that the toe of his shoe was behind it. That was all he needed. He pulled her the rest of the way out, and a moment later, the hole through which he'd gotten them both closed as the burning beam snapped in half. Tomaso came running back with two men. He picked up Jenna in his arms while the other two got Dario back into his chair and outside.

Jenna blinked several times before finally opening her eyes. She found herself looking up through a light rain into Dario's tender face. "Hello," he said quietly. "Welcome back."

"How did you get me out?"

"A little luck."

She moved, and for the first time realized that she was lying across Dario's lap in his chair. The stables were now completely engulfed in flames some twenty yards away.

She moved her head and coughed. Her throat ached.

"How do you feel?" he asked.

She wrinkled her nose in distaste. "Like I swallowed a lit cigarette."

Dario smiled and the arm around her shoulders hugged her closer. She turned her head and stared at the flames. "Did the horses get out all right?"

"They did."

She coughed again.

"You were a fool to go in there the way you did. No horse is worth your life."

"I wasn't thinking. I just couldn't stand listening to them in that fire without doing something about it."

"You just leap right into things, don't you?"

Her eyes met his. "I was very careful about falling in love with you, and look what it got me."

Isabella came running down from the house. "Dr. Madeiros is here as you asked, Dario," she panted, coming to a halt next to them and watching the flames.

Dario helped Jenna into a sitting position, and then onto her feet. "I want you to go back to the house with Isabella and let the doctor look at you. You were in the smoke for a long time."

"What about you?"

"I think I'll just stay here."

She paused. "Will I see you before I leave tomorrow?"

His eyes rested on her soot smudged face. "No."

Her heart contracted, but she inclined her head and, without another word, went back to the house with Isabella.

Chapter Ten

Jenna moved swiftly around the curtained rear of the hotel ballroom examining the models with a critical eye, straightening a belt here, lowering a sash there.

Christy finished sewing up a loose hem and ended up snapping off the thread with her teeth when she couldn't find her scissors. She stood next to Jenna and shook her head at the organized confusion. "Are we ready? Is it possible that we're actually ready?"

"We'd better be. The buyers are all here."

Soft rock with a bouncy beat started from the speakers and Jenna, looking like one of the models herself, glanced at her watch. "I have to get out there."

As she headed through the curtains to the podium where she was to announce the designs, Christy clapped her hands sharply. "All right, ladies. All of you in the first set line up. This is it."

Camera flashes went off in Jenna's face as she stepped

out and acknowledged the applause of the enthusiastic buyers. A film crew from a public station which wanted to cover the fashion show followed her. Jenna hated this part of her work, but the more exposure Hart-Windom got, the more their business grew. It seemed a fair trade.

Without any preliminaries, the first models stepped onto the runway, walking gracefully to the music, making the most of the clothes. Jenna announced design after design, explaining the uniqueness of some of the outfits as the models twirled and removed jackets.

For the first time in months, she wasn't thinking about Dario. This took all of her concentration.

The show was the best one ever, and when it was over, Jenna, Christy and Ken all collapsed onto a couch set up behind the curtains.

After awhile, Ken put his arm around Christy's shoulders and glanced at Jenna across the top of her head. "Want to go out to dinner with us?"

"No. I have to get home to Jamie. Mrs. Braun has plans for the evening and can't stay late."

"Bring him with you."

"I really don't want to," she said, smiling, "but thanks anyway."

Christy touched her friend's knee. "Jenna, why don't you just let the guy go? You've been half in another world ever since you got back from Portugal."

"The 'guy,' as you put it, is still my husband."

"In name only—and not even that much longer. When do the final papers come through."

"A few days."

"So celebrate! You'll be free."

"I don't want to be free. I want to be married to Dario Montoya."

"But he doesn't want you, Jenna, and you're going to have to face up to that or you'll go right over the edge."

A half smile curved Jenna's mouth. "Over what edge, Christy?"

"Oh, you know what I mean. Pining over this man isn't healthy."

She got to her feet. "Thank you both for your concern, but I'm fine, really. And believe me when I say I'm not near any dangerous edge. I'm a little depressed right now, but I'll get over it."

Christy and Ken shared a knowing look, but dropped it. "Are you coming into the office tomorrow?"

"I don't think so. As a matter of fact, I was thinking about taking Jamie off somewhere for a long weekend. I could use a little peace after this show. What about you two?"

"I have to come in," Ken said uncomplainingly. "The phones will be ringing off the hooks."

"I might as well come in, too," Christy said. "I haven't anything else to do."

"Then I'll see you both on Monday," Jenna told them and walked out into the early evening. It was half an hour drive to her new home and she enjoyed it. Traffic was light and spring was in the air. She turned onto the narrow road which led to her cozy three-bedroom house. Mrs. Braun smiled up at her when she walked in.

"How did the show go?"

Jenna tossed her keys onto the hall table. "We were a big hit. Where's Jamie?"

On cue, he came running in, an enchanting smile on his face. Jenna caught him in her arms and hugged him. Mrs. Braun collected her things and got ready to go.

"Do you want me to come tomorrow?"

"No. I think I'm going to take a few days off. I'm afraid I've neglected Jamie the last several weeks."

"What about next week?"

"I don't really know yet. Is it all right if I call you Sunday?"

"That's fine." She ruffled Jamie's dark head. "Goodbye, munchkin."

When Mrs. Braun had gone, Jenna sank onto the couch. Jamie struggled out of her arms and picked up a children's book on the floor, then brought it back to her and curled up on her lap. She kissed the top of his head and opened the book. He didn't want her to read it. He wanted her to say the names of the things he pointed at.

The doorbell rang. She didn't have the energy to get up. "It's open," she called, assuming that Christy and Ken had come to try to talk her into going out with them. They were amazingly persistent.

The door opened and after her initial shock, Jenna slowly rose to her feet. Dario stood there. Dario *stood* there.

A corner of his mouth lifted at the look on her face. "You could say hello."

Jamie walked over to him with a big smile. "Hi!" He bellowed one of his three words.

Dario leaned over and scooped up Jamie in one arm to kiss him. His other hand held a cane which he used to come the rest of the way into the room.

A tear slipped unnoticed down Jenna's smooth cheek. "Congratulations."

"Ah," he said to Jamie, "the fair maiden speaks."

"How did it happen?"

He sat down in a chair across from her and laid his cane on the floor. Jamie climbed onto his lap. It was as though he remembered him from all those months ago. Jenna sat down as well.

"Oddly enough, because of the stable fire. When I was getting you out, I used one of my legs—just a little—but enough to give me and the doctors hope that if I could do it once, I could do it again. I had some surgery right after you left Portugal and I've been going through the process of learning to walk for the past several months. The time will come when I won't even need the cane."

"I'm very happy for you." She couldn't believe the stilted words that came from her mouth when what she wanted to do was throw herself into his arms. She sat on her hands instead. "It was nice of you to come all this way to tell me."

His tawny eyes rested on her lovely face, hungry for the sight of her. "I've missed you and Jamie."

She licked her dry lips, at a loss for something to say. Then inspiration struck. "Can you stay for dinner?"

"What are you having?"

Jenna laughed with an adult for the first time in months.

"Of course I can stay for dinner," he said quietly. "I was hoping you'd offer."

"Would you have left if I hadn't?"

He shook his head. "Can't. I sent the taxi away."

Her smile reached her eyes. "I'll go to the kitchen to see what's there. I've been busy the past few weeks and grocery shopping hasn't been high on my list of priorities."

She walked into the kitchen and rummaged in the freezer. "I have some frozen steaks we can have later," she called out.

"Sounds fine," he called back.

She took them out and then got to work on Jamie's

dinner. It was almost his bedtime. Dario and Jamie came out to watch her. Jamie leaned against her leg and wrapped one arm around it while he quietly sucked his thumb, always a sure sign he was tired.

Dario watched the two of them with undisguised love. When she had the baby set up in his highchair, Dario stepped in. "May I feed him? It's been awhile."

Jenna handed him the spoon. Their hands accidentally brushed. She pulled hers back and held it against her. "I'll get his bath ready," she said and quickly left the kitchen.

Dario smiled down at Jamie. "Well, young fellow, I think she still loves me. What do you think?"

She came back ten minutes later. "Is he ready?"

Dario looked up guiltily and when Jenna saw Jamie, she knew why. He was covered forehead to lap with food, and loving it.

"He seemed to want to feed himself," Dario explained.

Jenna shook her head and gingerly picked up Jamie, holding him away from her as she took him into the bathroom.

Sometime later Jamie came running into the living room, flushed from his bath, his hair freshly washed, and naked as the day he was born. Dario laughed and picked him up. Jenna came running in after him, equally flushed, the front of her dress soaked. "Jammie time, young man."

"I think she means you," Dario told him.

Jamie clambered back down and over to Jenna. He wrapped his little hand around one of her fingers and they went off to his room. Dario followed and leaned against the doorframe as he watched.

In a few minutes he was diapered and put into his pajamas. Jenna handed him a small stuffed animal and pulled the blanket up around him. "Sweet dreams," she whispered, kissing his forehead. Then she walked to the door and flipped out the dim light.

"Is it like that every night?" Dario asked as they walked into the living room.

"Almost." She looked down at herself. "I think I'll change my clothes. I'm really not in the mood for drip-drying tonight."

While she was gone, Dario built a fire and then sat back to enjoy it. When Jenna returned, she had a bottle of wine and two glasses. "It's all I have," she apologized, setting it in front of him and then curling up in the chair across from him.

He stared into the fire and sighed. "I like this home, Jenna."

She looked around and smiled. "Thank you. I do, too. It's going to be a nice place for Jamie to grow up in, I think."

"There are no horses, though."

"And no bulls." Jenna said the words without thinking.

Dario's eyes touched her. The sun was setting and the living room was getting darker. "I understand Basilio and Isabella invited you to their wedding and you turned them down."

She leaned forward and picked up her glass of wine. "Yes, I did."

"Because of me?"

She took a sip and then held the glass cupped in both of her hands. "Because of us. I just didn't feel right about showing up for their wedding when our marriage was on the verge of ending."

"It's not until next week. You still have time to change your mind."

Jenna studied the man across from her. "Is that what this is all about? You want me to go to their wedding?"

"What I want is for you to come back to Portugal."

"Why?"

"Because I love you."

No one would have guessed the turmoil which suddenly raged through Jenna from the cool way she studied him. "I don't think I can live with your kind of love. You seem to think that the only time I deserve you is when you're whole, with no problems."

"You know what my reasons were for wanting you to live your own life away from me."

"I disagreed then, and I disagree now. I'm not some fair-weather lover, Dario. Or fair-weather wife. I was ready to handle whatever was ahead of us, but you wouldn't let me. You treated me like some child who didn't know what was best for her."

"I was wrong."

Jenna blinked. She had expected more of an argument.

"What?" he asked. "Silence?"

"You took the wind right out of my sails."

The room was now in darkness except for the firelight. "Do you still love me, Jenna?"

She rose abruptly. "I think I'll check on the steaks." She got all the way to the kitchen door, then stopped and looked at Dario over her shoulder. "Yes," she said almost in a whisper, but loud enough for the man on the couch to hear. "Yes, damn you."

When she didn't come back after a few minutes, Dario picked up his cane and went after her. The kitchen was dark except for the stove light. Jenna was standing there, both palms flat on the counter, her golden head bent. "Jenna?"

She straightened and dashed at her cheeks with the back of her hand before efficiently poking one of the steaks with a fork. "I'm afraid it's going to be awhile yet."

He eyed her quietly. "It's all right. I'm not really hungry."

"Well I am." She started to open the refrigerator door, but Dario put his hand on it and held it closed. Jenna just stood there pulling on it and pulling on it, until she finally stopped and leaned her forehead against the door.

Dario set his cane aside and turned her into his arms. "It's all right, Jenna."

Suddenly her face crumpled. She clutched the front of his shirt in her hands and buried her face in his neck as he held her against him, wrapped in his arms. She cried quietly, which Dario found all the more heartrending. "I'm sorry, Jenna," he whispered against her hair. "I never meant to hurt you like this. I wanted you to be happy."

She let go of his shirt and wrapped her arms around his neck in a deathlike grip. "I could never be happy without you. How could you not know that?" she hiccoughed.

"I am an idiot." He buried his face in her hair and breathed the fragrance he had come to love. "Jenna, you are as much a part of me as my heartbeat. You have been since the first time I saw you."

Jenna moved away from him a little and raised her eyes to his. "Then I *was* the woman you loved when you married Elisa."

"You are the only woman I've ever loved," he said quietly. "When I came here after Elisa's death, it wasn't just to get Jamie. It was to get you. I was going to take you back to my home and have you fall in love with me."

She smiled. "Your plan worked."

"And then fell apart. I honestly thought I wasn't going to make it through the surgery. By making you my wife, I was seeing that you and our child, if you carried him, would be protected, and that Jamie would get his due as a Montoya through you. I can't tell you how I felt when I realized I was going to live—and that I had stuck you with a cripple." His hands cupped her face. "My beautiful, passionate Jenna. I couldn't bear to look at you."

Jenna's mouth closed over Dario's and she molded her body against his. He groaned as he pulled her even more tightly against him. He was hungry for her, this woman he loved beyond reason.

"You realize," he whispered against her ear, "that our annullment will never go through if we do what we're about to."

"Only if we tell." She moved seductively against him and Dario caught his breath sharply.

"I have to." He smiled down into her eyes. "As you've told me so often, I'm an honorable man."

Epilogue

It was the weekend. The day after a show. The office was a noisy flurry of activity. The telephones had been ringing all morning. One line rang and rang and finally Christy pushed the flashing light at the bottom and lifted the receiver. "Just a minute," she finally said. "Jenna! Pick up line three, wherever you are! It's your doctor."

Jenna poked her head around her office door, ten yards away. "My doctor?"

"That's right." She was scribbling on a sheet of paper while she held the phone cradled on her neck. "You should see the order we just got from Degas Sportswear. Triple what they ordered last year."

But Jenna had already gone back into her office and closed the door. She sat behind her desk and stared at the phone a minute before lifting the receiver to her ear. "Hello, Dr. Kelly."

"Jenna, at last. How are you, dear?"

"How about if you tell me the answer to that."

She could hear the smile in his voice and the muscles in her stomach relaxed. "It will be my pleasure. You're pregnant."

A soft smile curved her mouth. "Thank you," she whispered.

"Don't thank me. Thank your husband."

Jenna choked on her laugh. "I'll do that."

"When are you going back to Portugal? I'd like to make sure your doctor there has your medical history."

"I'm supposed to leave here in a week. I've already been gone for two weeks."

"That's a long time."

"Too long."

"Well, have a safe trip and give me a call on your next visit."

Jenna hung up the phone and leaned back in her chair. She rested her hand lightly on her stomach and smiled again.

Christy walked into her office, her attention on her order forms. "You might want to go over these later. We picked up several new buyers this time out."

"All right."

There was something in Jenna's voice that captured Christy's attention. She looked at her partner—really looked at her—for the first time since walking in, then put the order forms on the desk and sat down across from her. "What happened?"

"I'm going to have a baby."

Christy's face lit up. "She reached across the desk and clasped her friend's hands. "That's wonderful! Does Dario know yet?"

She shook her head. "I haven't called him."

"This isn't something you should tell him over the phone."

"It's either that or burst trying to hold the news to myself for another week."

"So go home now and tell him."

"Christy, I'm only here for a few weeks a year as it is. I feel guilty about leaving early."

"Nonsense," Christy affectionately reprimanded her. "You and I both know what your priorities are. Your family comes first, and that's as it should be—as long as you keep coming up with those wonderful designs of yours. The extra people we hired last year can handle whatever you don't finish before going back to Portugal."

"Are you sure?"

"We'll manage, believe me."

Jenna came around the desk and hugged her friend. "Oh, Christy, I'm so happy."

Christy hugged her back. "And I'm happy for you. I know how much the two of you want children. Now, go on, get out of here and get packed. There must be some plane or other going to Lisbon this afternoon."

Jenna raced home and packed some of the clothes she kept in Chicago, then went to the airport and less than two hours later she was on her way to Dario.

The flight was a long one, and for the first time she found herself a little queasy, but even that made her smile. It was just another sign of the baby. Dario's baby.

She had to rent a car at the Lisbon airport for the drive home. It was nearly two in the morning when she pulled up in front of the villa.

Trying not to make any noise, she climbed the stairs to their bedroom and found Dario asleep. She stood quietly looking down at him, loving him so much it brought tears to her eyes. She leaned over, her face close to his. Dario slowly opened his eyes, sensing her presence, and a slow smile curved his handsome mouth. "Am I dreaming again, or are you really here?"

Her mouth covered his and his strong arms went around her slender body, pulling her into bed with him. "Ummmm," he sighed after a moment. "You're really here. You should have called. I would have picked you up."

"I wanted to surprise you."

His hand cupped her cheek as they lay facing one another, his eyes tender. "I've missed you."

She kissed him again and pressed her body against his. Dario's response was instant and she felt him hard against her. There was no need for preliminaries. They just wanted each other with a raw passion that had grown rather than decreased since their marriage eighteen months earlier.

Afterwards they lay facing each other again. Dario's eyes roamed over her face. "I love you," he said softly. "It amazes me sometimes, how deeply I love you." He took her face in his hands and tenderly kissed her. "My Jenna. Why are you home a week early?"

"I couldn't bear to be away from you any longer—and I had some news that couldn't wait." She took his hand and placed it on her still flat stomach. "Dario, I'd like you to meet the newest member of the Montoya family."

He looked at her for a long moment. They had been trying for over a year to have a child and had begun to think that perhaps they couldn't. Suddenly, as Jenna was trying to figure out what his reaction was, he slid down the bed and lay on top of her, his chest on her legs, his arms wrapped around her hips. His mouth gently brushed her stomach and then he rested his cheek on it. Jenna reached out and touched his thick hair. His simple action told her more than words could have.

After a few minutes he slid back up so that they were face to face. His mouth slowly caressed hers and Jenna felt a delicious warmth rising in her body. "Just when I think I can't love you any more," he said, "I find I do."

Jenna wrapped her arms around him and ran her hands over his smoothly muscled back, wanting him all over again.

"Will this hurt the child?" he asked.

A smile curved her mouth. "According to the doctor, you can have your way with me for another six months."

He pushed the silky hair away from her face. "Then I hope you've had a lot of sleep. This one is going to take awhile."

He wrapped his arms around her and they held each other quietly for a moment. Jenna closed her eyes and buried her face in his neck and let the warmth of his body flow into her. It still amazed her. Of all the women in the world, she was the one this man had chosen to love.

Of all the men in the world, she had found the one who was just right for her.

READERS' COMMENTS ON SILHOUETTE ROMANCES:

"The best time of my day is when I put my children to bed at naptime and sit down to read a Silhouette Romance. Keep up the good work."

P.M.*, Allegan, MI

"I am very fond of the quality of your Silhouette Romances. They are so real. I have tried to read some of the other romances, but I always come back to Silhouette."

C.S., Mechanicsburg, PA

"I feel that Silhouette Books offer a wider choice and/or variety than any of the other romance books available."

R.R., Aberdeen, WA

"I have enjoyed reading Silhouette Romances for many years now. They are light and refreshing. You can always put yourself in the main characters' place, feeling alive and beautiful."

J.M.K., San Antonio, TX

"My boyfriend always teases me about Silhouette Books. He asks me, how's my love life and naturally I say terrific, but I tell him that there is always room for a little more romance from Silhouette."

F.N., Ontario, Canada

*names available on request

Four exciting
First Love from Silhouette
romances yours for 15 days—*free!*

These are the books that girls everywhere are reading and talking about, the most popular teen novels being published today. They're about things that matter most to young women, with stories that mirror their innermost thoughts and feelings, and characters so real they seem like friends.

To show you how special First Love from Silhouette is, we'd like to send you or your daughter four exciting books to look over for 15 days—absolutely free—as an introduction to the First Love from Silhouette Book Club.℠ If you enjoy them as much as we believe you will, keep them and pay the invoice enclosed with your trial shipment. Or return them at no charge.

As a member of the Club, you will get First Love from Silhouette books regularly—delivered right to your home. Four new books every month for only $1.95 each. You'll always be among the first to get them, and you'll never miss a title. There are never any delivery charges and you're under no obligation to buy anything at any time. Plus, as a special bonus, you'll receive a *free* subscription to the First Love from Silhouette Book Club newsletter!

So don't wait. To receive your four books, fill out and mail the coupon below *today!*

First Love from Silhouette is a service mark and registered trademark.